THE TORN NOTE

AF603905

TARANJIET SINGH NAMDHARI

INDIA • SINGAPORE • MALAYSIA

Copyright © Taranjiet Singh Namdhari 2023
All Rights Reserved.

ISBN 979-8-88935-321-8

This book has been published with all efforts taken to make the material error-free after the consent of the author. However, the author and the publisher do not assume and hereby disclaim any liability to any party for any loss, damage, or disruption caused by errors or omissions, whether such errors or omissions result from negligence, accident, or any other cause.

While every effort has been made to avoid any mistake or omission, this publication is being sold on the condition and understanding that neither the author nor the publishers or printers would be liable in any manner to any person by reason of any mistake or omission in this publication or for any action taken or omitted to be taken or advice rendered or accepted on the basis of this work. For any defect in printing or binding the publishers will be liable only to replace the defective copy by another copy of this work then available.

for

my wife Bandna Preet Kaur

my son Pyaaraa Singh Namdhari

my parents and grand parents

Contents

Acknowledgements

I would like to express my sincere gratitude to Satguru Jagjit Singh Ji and Satguru Uday Singh Ji, who has inspired me in every sphere of my life and have always encouraged me to be open to all the possibilities that the Universe has to offer. Their positivity and guidance have had a profound impact on my thinking, and I am grateful for the role they have played in helping me to focus on the good and follow my heart with honesty and pride.

To my wife, Bandna Preet Kaur, for her unwavering support and invaluable feedback throughout the writing process. The first person to hear as well as read my work in progress. She has been my rock, my ardent critic, and my support system as I pursued my dream of being an independent creative professional. Thank you for always believing in me and being there, even when others thought we should take a different path. Here's to many more shared journeys to come.

I also want to thank my son, Pyaaraa Singh Namdhari, for his encouragement and enthusiasm for my writing. It means a lot to me that he has been urging me to write a novel, or rather an interesting storybook as he says, for years now.

Finally, I am indebted to KV Ramesh and Pankaja Srinivasan for their guidance on the book publishing process through our conversations. Their insights were invaluable.

Chapter 1

Jia

It was as mundane a day as it could get. A slight breeze blew the leaves lying bare on the unkempt common society ground in front of the small, independent house in suburban Chembur. Several bikes were parked out front. Inside the house, an irritated Jia, dressed in her usual white shorts and red t-shirt, fiddled with the oven in an attempt to get it working for her next order. The cupcake batter had been sitting for a while now, and if she didn't get it in the oven soon, it wouldn't be ready on time. The looped clamour of a medical insurance advertisement blared in the background, grating on her nerves.

Nandu, her next-door neighbour and current live-in boyfriend, sat at his keyboard, composing music for the advertisement when the phone started ringing. He had charmed Jia with his cool demeanour and music when her marriage with her estranged husband, Gaurav, had strained. She had found solace in his music and words then, but now she could neither tolerate his music nor his company. Jia had decided she would suffer him only until her business loan was paid off. There were still four instalments to go. Nandu's voice broke into her thoughts.

"Jia, your phone is ringing," he called out to her.

"Pick it up," Jia replied, not taking her eyes off the oven.

"I'm busy," Nandu said, his fingers flying over the keys.

"Then what is my phone doing with you?" Jia asked, frustration creeping into her voice.

Nandu refused to pick up the phone and continued working. The phone stopped ringing, but then started to ring again a few moments later. This time, Nandu answered it.

"Who is this?" Nandu asked.

A heavily accented Gujrati voice on the other end of the line squeaked. "*Sanket, che bhai*. Your order is ready. Please come and collect it."

Nandu was confused. He looked around to see if Jia could overhear and shouted into the phone, "I didn't order anything. This must be a wrong number." He hung up the phone.

The phone rang again a few moments later. "*Sanket, che bhai...Ga...*" Sanket said.

“I already told you, it’s the wrong number,” Nandu cut in sternly.

“There’s always risk in our business. Don’t be pissed off *bhai*?” Sanket replied.

“Listen, buddy, I’m not interested in your ‘*bhai*’. I didn’t order anything. You dialled the wrong number. Got it? And if you call again, I will personally come and give you a taste of risk in your business,” Nandu said before hanging up the phone.

Jia entered the room and asked, “What’s going on? Why are you shouting?”

“Wrong number,” Nandu replied, waving his hand dismissively.

“Wrong number? That’s it? Do you have any idea what I have to deal with? Aunty has taken the day off again, and the oven isn’t working. How am I supposed to get those orders done? And what happened to my masalas? You were supposed to go and get them the day before yesterday,” Jia asked, anger creeping into her voice.

“I’ll order them online, yaar. Some guy named Sanket was on the line saying the order was ready and wanted me to come and collect it,” Nandu retorted back.

“Must be the food containers that I had ordered; I still have to pay for the earlier order, but I need the containers," she shrugged and said as a matter of fact. She turned to go back into the kitchen when the phone rang again. Nandu picked it up and was about to curse into it when Jia snatched the phone from him and answered it herself. "Hello, Ghanshyam *bhai*?"

"Hello, madam, how are you? It's Sanket. What's happened to Gaurav *bhai*?" Sanket asked.

"Sanket? Who Sanket?" Jia asked.

"Don't you remember me, madam? It's Sanket, Sanket Patel, Madhav *bhai's* man" Sanket replied.

Jia thought for a moment and then realisation dawned on her. "Sanket... Madhav *bhai's* man?" she asked.

"Yes, madam, it's me. How are you?" Sanket replied.

"I'm fine. What do you want?" Jia asked.

"I just wanted to check in and see how you and Gaurav *bhai* are doing," Sanket said.

"We're fine. How are you?" Jia asked, trying to keep the conversation brief.

"I'm good, madam. I've been thinking about you and Gaurav *bhai* a lot lately. I wanted to apologise for any trouble I may have caused you in the past," Sanket apologetic.

"It's okay. It's in the past now" Jia's voice trailed off as she went a couple of years back.

It was 2020. She had been living with her husband Gaurav Sinha in this very house. The house belonged to Gaurav only that now they were separated and she was living in with their neighbour and Gaurav's friend Nandu Dias.

Gaurav used to work as a collection and delivery agent for Madhav bhai, a wheeler-dealer who ran a credit card collection call centre by the day and moved huge sums of money and jewellery for several people through the angadia system, the informal banking system. Sanket Patel had been his point man. Gaurav's job was to deliver and collect parcels on behalf of Madhav bhai. He was a 'kabootar', or delivery pigeon, as Madhav called him humorously.

She remembered that day clearly, the oven had been delivered the same day, it was their first purchase for the cloud kitchen which she was setting up from home.

Gaurav had tried to call Sanket since the morning, but his phone had been turned off. He had returned Gaurav's call in the afternoon. It was bad news. There had been a rash of police raids in recent months, and Sanket had been raided that day. Gaurav would earn the promised commission only if he was able to collect the parcel and deliver it to Madhav's wife. With Jia and Gaurav having poured their savings into her cloud kitchen, life had already been difficult, and now with Sanket raided, Gaurav was in trouble. If something went awry, Madhav was known to reclaim the parcel money from his 'pigeon's' pay checks or personal assets.

"Hello madam, *aap line pe ho*?" squeaked Sanket

Jia's thoughts were brought back to the present as she stared at the phone in her hand. She was surprised to receive a call from Sanket, who hadn't called in two years, and realised that the number used to belong to Gaurav before they separated. Thank goodness Nandu hadn't noticed, or it could have led to another argument, something Jia could do without.

"Hey Sanket, I'm here. It's been two years. What's up?" she asked, her curiosity getting the better of her.

"Madam, the police had invited me to have tea with them at the police station, and I just got back home yesterday. Come and collect your parcel, and *haan* don't forget the payment" Sanket replied.

Jia realised she couldn't talk in front of Nandu, so she told Sanket she would call him back in a few minutes. She hung up the phone with a sigh and got up to go into the kitchen.

Nandu scoffed at her and said, "Who was it? You owe somebody again?"

Jia glared at him and went into the kitchen, taking the phone with her. Inside the kitchen, she looked at the oven and then at her phone. With a sigh, she called Sanket back and asked, "Hello Sanket, you were saying something..."

"I was saying that you should come and collect your parcel," Sanket repeated.

"Parcel?" Jia asked, confused.

"Madam, you know I can't say much over the phone. Gaurav *bhai* knows about it. Come today. Okay?" Sanket said.

"Okay," Jia replied, relieved to have received some good news after so long. "But how do I get rid of this bloody idiot?" she thought to herself, glancing at Nandu scratching himself outside in the hall. He noticed her watching and sheepishly smiled. With a shake of her head, she came out and threw an empty carry bag at Nandu, saying, "Stop scratching."

Nandu replied, "Hey, my fingers are sore after all that playing."

Jia rolled her eyes and said, "Whatever. Do me a favour and go to Parel and get me my masalas. Go quickly."

Nandu asked, "Masalas? From Parel?"

Parel was not only Jia's but also Mumbai's favourite haunt for shopping for spices. There were all kinds of fresh spices to be bought there. Jia loved shopping there, but Nandu hated going there. He had an allergy. The smell of fresh masalas being pounded and the heady smell of the mix in the air always sent him into a sneezing delirium.

"I want fresh masalas, which you were supposed to go and get before," Jia explained, her frustration with Nandu's forgetfulness mounting. "And if we're going to get the orders done on time, we need them now."

An annoyed Nandu looked at Jia and said, "Why can't we order online? You might have forgotten, but they have an online portal. I can order for you. They will deliver within an hour. I have work to do." He took out his phone.

Jia grabbed him by the collar and said, "Do as I say, Nandu, or I'll make the masala out of you." She pushed him out of the house and closed the door.

As soon as Nandu left, Jia unlocked her phone and called Sanket. "Sanket, it's me," she said.

"Yes, madam. What time can you come?" Sanket asked.

"Where do I need to come?" Jia asked.

"I'll ping you the location map. And don't forget the '*note*'. You need to bring that as payment. Don't forget," Sanket said.

"Okay," Jia replied. "Sanket, listen, it's been two years. I don't remember where I put that '*note*'. Can you deliver without it?"

"Madam, you know I can't give you the parcel without the '*note*'. It's okay; you can search for it and call me back on this number when you find it. But do it quickly. I'm leaving Mumbai for good in three days," Sanket said before hanging up the phone.

Jia put the phone down and thought to herself. She walked into the bedroom, feeling a sense of determination as she approached her wardrobe. She opened the doors and began rummaging through the files kept under the clothes, searching for the '*note*'. But as she looked, she realised that it wasn't there. Frustrated, she sat down on the bed and tried to remember where Gaurav had kept it.

On a hunch, she made her way to the small storeroom where they kept all their random belongings. She rummaged through boxes and piles of books and paperwork but still couldn't find anything. She let out a sigh of frustration and sat down. And then, in a sudden moment of clarity, she remembered where she had last seen the frame. Flashes of memory came flooding back to her.

Her mind pictured *Gaurav placing the 'note' inside their wedding photo frame*. But where did he keep the frame?

Chapter 2

Gaurav

Jia remembered the day she threw Gaurav out of the house.

He had pleaded with her, desperately trying to persuade her to let him stay, but she remained steadfast in her decision. "Get out of here," she said firmly. "I don't want to listen to any more of your excuses. You should have thought about this before spending all my money on her."

Gaurav insisted that he was going to get it back, but Jia wasn't satisfied. "You believe you will get it back?" she said coldly. "Have you ever thought of doing anything worthwhile?"

"She needed help and had nowhere else to go," Gaurav replied, desperation in his voice.

But Jia was unconvinced. "Now, you can go and live with her," she said dismissively. "Just leave."

In the background, Nandu watched the scene unfold with a smug smile on his face. Gaurav, filled with anger and frustration, turned on Nandu, blaming him for his and Jia's breakup.

"You son of a gun," Gaurav yelled. "This is all your fault. I know, you have had an eye on her from the day she moved in"

Nandu, unfazed, retorted, "Hey loser, don't blame me. I didn't do charity with her money or forget that it was for setting up her business."

The confrontation escalated into a scuffle, but Jia stepped in to stop them. "Stop it, both of you," she said firmly.

Gaurav, panting and angry, yelled at Nandu, "I won't let you get away with this."

But Nandu wasn't intimidated and teased him. "I won't let you get away with this. Come, let's decide this once and for all, face to face."

Gaurav snarled, "You son of a..."

Jia interrupted him, "Gaurav, leave. I said just leave."

Jia sighed deeply as she pulled out her phone. She scrolled through her contacts until she found Gaurav's name, hesitating for a moment before unblocking him. She dialled his number.

Gaurav was washing dishes in the kitchen when the phone rang. He looked at the phone and noticed it was Jia calling. He stopped to wipe his hands with a cloth before picking up, but the phone stopped ringing before he could answer.

Knowing Gaurav's desperate desire to talk to her, Jia had expected him to answer the phone immediately. She frowned in frustration at the continuous ringing, and eventually hung up, staring at the phone in anger.

After a moment of contemplation, she decided to call again. The phone rang a few times before Gaurav finally answered.

"Hi Gaurav," Jia said.

Gaurav stared at the phone, stunned for a moment at hearing Jia's voice after such a long time.

"Hello? Are you there?" Jia's voice came through the phone. Gaurav immediately collected himself and replied.

"Yes, yes, honey, I'm here. I can't believe you called. I had given up hope of hearing your lovely voice, I mean, I'm shocked! What do I owe this generosity to?"

"Shut up," Jia snapped sarcastically. "Looks like you're doing just fine without me."

"Well, ever since you left me, it's been fantastic. Things are looking up actually," Gaurav said. "Sometimes I wonder why you didn't just kick me out of the house earlier."

"I know," Jia replied. "That's why I had to block your number."

"So why unblock me now?" Gaurav asked. "Looks like you're bored of our dear neighbour, or have you had a change of heart?"

"Listen, Gaurav," Jia said, trying to keep the frustration out of her voice. "I have something important to talk to you about."

"Talk to me?" Gaurav replied, surprised. "Since when have I become so important? What do you want?"

"Some of my stuff is missing," Jia explained. "Maybe you took it with you when you left."

"I took it?" Gaurav asked, incredulous. "Jia, let me remind you, you kicked me out of the house and packed my stuff yourself. What are you looking for anyway?"

"Our wedding photo frame," Jia replied, feeling a sense of desperation. "The one that *bhaiya* had gifted us; I want it back."

"Seriously, a photo frame..." Gaurav said, unable to hide his sarcasm. "That's a good excuse. Honestly, what are you looking for?"

"I'm serious, Gaurav," Jia insisted. "Please, I need that frame back."

"Jia, I don't have a photo of ours together, forget a framed photograph," Gaurav said, his tone harsh. "Put the phone down and do something productive."

Jia cursed silently as she hung up the phone in frustration, pacing the room and trying to come up with a plan. She glanced at her phone, contemplating whether to call Gaurav again. As anger welled up inside her, she took a deep breath and tried Gaurav's number again. With bated breath, she waited for him to pick up, her mind racing for a way to avoid completely losing her temper. And then Gaurav's voice filtered into the phone "Hello..."

Just as she was about to speak, the sound of Nandu's motorcycle pulling up outside caught her attention. She watched through the window as he approached the door and rang the bell, her heart sinking as she disconnected the call.

She took a deep breath and opened the door, greeting Nandu with a forced smile. She couldn't help but feel angry and frustrated at having to disconnect the call.

She had hoped that Nandu would, as usual, take his time and stay away longer, that he had an allergic attack and needed time to recover before coming home, giving her time to find out where the photo frame was. But now, there he was, standing in front of her, demanding her attention and loyalty.

Meanwhile, after finishing the dishes, Gaurav was lost in memories as he pulled out a suitcase from under the bed and opened it. Beneath a few clothes, he found a half-torn album with photos from his wedding to Jia, and a twinge of loss and longing washed over him. He couldn't help but think about the events that had led him to this point.

He remembered how he and Jia had met at Madhav bhai's daughter's wedding. She was working for the food caterer, and Gaurav was handling Madhav bhai's accounting with the vendors. With big brown eyes and short hair tied in a bun dressed smartly in a bright yellow sleeveless crop top with denim shorts, Jia Sharma was all business-like and professional. But Gaurav couldn't take his eyes off her. He had fallen head over heels for her.

"You're staring," Jia said, catching him looking at her.

Gaurav blushed. "I'm sorry. You just caught my eye."

Jia laughed. "It's okay. I'm flattered."

Gaurav seized the opportunity. "By the way, I heard you're from Delhi Catering College. My cousin Sana studied there, too."

"Oh really?" Jia said, intrigued. "What's she up to now?"

"She's running her own catering business," Gaurav said, proud of his cousin. "She's a real go-getter."

"I bet," Jia said, impressed. "What about you?"

"Oh, I'm just the gofer," Gaurav said, waving his hand dismissively. "But I'm working on it. I'm saving up to start my own business one day."

"I have a feeling you'll get there," Jia said, smiling.

Gaurav did everything he could to woo Jia throughout the various events. At the mehndi, he offered to help her with the henna cones and made sure to brush his fingers against hers whenever he could.

"Your hands are so soft," Gaurav whispered, gazing into Jia's eyes.

Jia blushed. "I moisturise a lot."

"It's worth it," Gaurav said, grinning. "I bet you have the most kissable lips, too."

Jia's eyes widened. "Gaurav!"

"What? It's true," Gaurav said, shrugging innocently.

At the sangeet, he asked her to dance and held her close, stealing kisses whenever the music slowed down.

"You're a great dancer," Jia said, resting her head on Gaurav's shoulder.

"You make it easy," Gaurav replied, pressing his lips to her forehead. "And you're the most beautiful woman in the room."

Jia rolled her eyes playfully. "Flattery will get you everywhere."

By the time the wedding was over, they were already planning their own. Though not the quintessential prince charming, Gaurav was funny, smart, and honest – a virtue that Madhav bhai placed a premium on when he hired anyone. And Gaurav was his blue-eyed boy.

Jia moved in with Gaurav and six months later they were married. The house had belonged to Gaurav's elder brother Ranjit, who had passed away a year before. Gaurav's Bhabhi - Kala, along with her young son Ajit and teenage daughter Seema, had shifted to her mother's place. Kala would visit them occasionally and Gaurav would help her out financially.

One day, Kala came to visit Gaurav and found him unpacking a suitcase, with Jia standing nearby. "Hey, Gaurav," Kala said. "What are you doing?"

"Oh, just going through some old stuff," Gaurav replied. "I found this album with photos from your wedding. I was just showing it to Jia."

Kala sat down next to them and looked at the photos. "We used to be so happy," she looked at Jia said. "I'm glad you found someone who makes you happy, Gaurav. It's not easy to move on after losing someone you love."

Jia smiled and squeezed Gaurav's hand. "I'm grateful to have Gaurav by my side, too," she said. "I'm sorry I never had the chance to meet your husband, Ranjit."

"I know," Kala said, sighing. "I miss him every day. But I'm glad Ajit and Seema have you and Gaurav to look up to. Seema is already studying in Bangalore, and Ajit is going to join her there soon. The tuition and hostel fees are so expensive, though. I don't know how we'll manage."

Gaurav immediately reached for his wallet. "Don't worry, Bhabhi. I'll help you out. Just let me know how much you need."

Jia noticed the exchange but didn't say anything. She knew how much Gaurav cared about his family, and she didn't want to resent him for it.

Gaurav continued working at Madhav bhai's call centre and also ran personal errands for him. Madhav bhai trusted him immensely and would often send Gaurav to pick up special parcels from various Angadia's in Mumbai.

Then the police raids started, and the government declared a moratorium on loan collections by agents. The Supreme Court ordered that there would be no cash interest collected on loans. Banks were ordered to be more customer friendly and go digital. Non-banking cash transactions, like the ones carried out by Madhav bhai's call centre, were greatly affected.

As a result, Madhav bhai was forced to lay off most of his staff, including Gaurav, who struggled to find work in the digital fin-tech world and his financial struggles and frustration put a strain on his relationship with Jia.

Gaurav pulled out his phone and opened the photos app. Scrolling through his and Jia's photos, he couldn't help but notice the ones with Nandu in them.

Their neighbour, Nandu Dias, was a budding YouTube musician. Gaurav remembered Nandu's jealousy and resentment towards him, and how he had used their conflicts to drive a wedge between them. He offered Jia a shoulder to lean on whenever they fought, listening to her vent and using the opportunity to build his relationship with her. This ultimately led to Gaurav and Jia's separation.

Shortly after Jia and Gaurav separated, Nandu moved in intending to marry her as soon as their divorce was finalised.

Gaurav couldn't help but wonder if there was still a chance for him and Jia to repair their relationship. However, with Nandu there, he knew it wouldn't be easy. He wasn't even sure if he was willing to confront the man who had caused so much misery in his life again.

He drifted off to sleep abusing Nandu only to be rudely awakened by the sound of the phone ringing again. He groggily picked it up, still half asleep. "Hmm," he muttered.

"Gaurav, did you find that photo frame?" it was Jia again on the other end.

He let out a loud yawn. "Are you serious? You've been asking for that stupid photo frame since morning. I guess I threw it away. I have no idea where it is," he replied irritably.

"Gaurav, you idiot! You're such a fool..." Jia scolded him and hung up.

Gaurav stared at the phone in frustration before getting up from the bed and stretching.

Chapter 3

The Frame

After his separation from Jia, Gaurav had moved into a tiny one-room flat owned by one of Madhav *bhai's* acquaintances. Jia had also stayed there in the early days of their courtship. Gaurav had the flat to himself for the next six months, until the acquaintance returned from his overseas trip. He knew he not only needed to quickly find another place to stay but some work as well, to pay for everything.

As he shaved, Gaurav couldn't help but wonder why Jia was calling him so insistently about the photo frame. He was certain it wasn't out of love. He racked his brain, trying to figure out what was going on. He replayed Jia's conversation in his mind.

Jia's voice echoed in his head: "Gaurav, did you find that photo frame?"

Gaurav stopped shaving and answered, "I threw it away." He laughed, but Jia's voice, laced with anger, rang in his head. "*Gaurav, you idiot! You moron...*"

From earlier times, the voice rang again in his mind: "You idiot! You moron..."

Jia was angry. She was running the house with her kitchen, but she needed money to scale up deliveries. However, Gaurav had been laid off, and he was desperately trying to find new work. They were struggling to make ends meet. He went back to Madhav bhai.

"Madhav bhai, please, please give me some work. I'm broke..." he pleaded.

Madhav bhai coughed profousely as he replied, "Everyone's in the same boat. Do one thing: open a delivery service. Your wife cooks, you should deliver. You'll make a great team."

Gaurav responded, "Madhav bhai, how can I start a delivery service? I don't even have money to buy a bike. Look, you must have something for me..."

Madhav bhai sighed as he wiped his lips with a handkerchief. "Hmmm... Now you're begging. Come home tomorrow. Enter through the back gate."

Gaurav heaved a sigh of relief as Madhav finally relented. The next day when he met Madhav bhai at his house, he gave Gaurav a torn 'note', asking him to exchange it for a parcel from Sanket.

"Here, take this. Give it to Sanket and get the parcel from him. Take it to my wife in Thane. You'll get two per cent of the value on delivery," Madhav bhai instructed.

Gaurav replied, "bhai, please make it five per cent."

Madhav bhai snapped, coughing again, "Do you want work or not, you moron?"

Gaurav had tried calling Sanket throughout the morning, but his phone was switched off. When Sanket called back in the afternoon, Gaurav heard the bad news.

"Hello, Sanket bhai. I was supposed to pick up the parcel..."

"Gaurav bhai... I'm in a jam. The government has prohibited the angadias from operating, and the police have cracked down on us. We've been raided," Sanket's voice came through the phone.

"And now?" Gaurav asked.

"I don't know. I would suggest you also leave town for a few days..." Sanket replied.

Gaurav overheard a chorus of voices in the background shouting, "Close the shop! Run, run, the police are coming!" Then, the call was disconnected abruptly.

Gaurav looked at a worried Jia, who asked, "What now?" He dialled Madhav bhai's number, feeling a sense of urgency. He knew that Madhav bhai was waiting, and he couldn't afford to waste any time. As the phone rang, Gaurav paced back and forth in his living room, trying to come up with a plan.

Finally, Madhav answered the phone, his voice sounding strained and laboured. "Gaurav, I'm in the hospital; I've had an asthma attack," he gasped.

Gaurav's heart sank. "Madhav bhai, what can I do?" he asked, desperation creeping into his voice. "Sanket has been arrested by the police. I don't know how to get the parcel now."

He heard Madhav let out a sigh, his breathing becoming shallower as he coughed hard. His wife's voice filtered in from the left: "Hey, he can't even catch his breath right now. And you're worried about a parcel? Please don't bother him right now."

Gaurav felt a pang of guilt wash over him. Here he was, worried about money, while Madhav was fighting for his life. "I'm sorry," he said quietly, hanging up the phone.

But Madhav had already disconnected the call, leaving Gaurav alone with his thoughts and fears. He tried calling both Sanket and Madhav back over the next few days, but neither of them answered. Gaurav's mind raced with worry as he tried to figure out what to do next. The only way was to hold on until Sanket resurfaced. But he hadn't;

A couple of days later, Gaurav found out that Sanket had been arrested and sent to judicial remand. He had been denied bail, and no one knew when he would be back. His life went into a tizzy when, a few days later, he heard that Madhav bhai had also passed away. He looked around and took their wedding photo frame from the mantle. He opened the frame and hid the torn note between their wedding photo and the white background paper. He knew they were in a mess.

Gaurav wiped his face clean with the back of his hand, finally understanding why Jia had been calling him. He guessed that Sanket was probably back, and he would have called. Perhaps there was still time for some redemption. He picked up his phone and scrolled through his contacts, searching for Sanket's number. He dialled, only to be informed by a recorded voice that the number did not exist anymore.

Gaurav cursed under his breath and thought for a moment before deciding to call an old colleague of his, Shantanu.

"Shanky," Gaurav said into the phone.

"Who?" Shantanu's voice came through the speaker.

"It's Gaurav," he replied.

"*Arre*, Gaurav *bhai*. How are you?" Shantanu asked.

"I'm fine. Hey, do you remember Sanket?" Gaurav asked. "Do you know where he is these days?"

"Sanket? Who?" Shantanu asked.

"Sanket Patel," Gaurav said.

"Oh, Patel. Yeah, I remember him. Let me see if I can find out where he is," Shantanu said.

A few minutes later, Shantanu called back. "Gaurav *bhai*, I heard that he'd been locked up in jail. He just got bail a week ago, but I don't know where he is now," Shantanu said.

Gaurav thanked him, and a plan began to form in his mind. "Thanks, Shanky. I owe you a drink," Gaurav said.

"A drink? Gaurav *bhai*, just a drink won't help. You owe me a good old bottle of Old monk," Shantanu replied with a laugh before hanging up.

Back at home, Jia was busy working on her next order in the kitchen when the phone rang again. Nandu picked it up and was just about to answer when Jia snatched it away and went out to the veranda to take the call. The voice on the other end, Sanket, was urgent, asking for Gaurav.

“Hey, Sanket?” Jia greeted him cheerfully.

“Jia, where’s Gaurav?” Sanket asked urgently. “I’ve been trying to reach you for hours.”

“I’m not sure,” Jia replied hesitantly, uncertain about how to tell Sanket the truth about their relationship. “I haven’t seen him since your last call. We’re still trying to find that *note*.”

“I need to speak with him as soon as possible,” Sanket said, his voice laced with desperation. “I’m leaving Mumbai in a few hours and I need to know if he is coming to collect the parcel?”

“I understand, but can’t you wait a little longer?” Jia asked, trying to stand her ground. “We haven’t had much luck finding the ‘*note*’ yet. I promise I’ll call you back as soon as we find it.”

“I need to leave as soon as possible,” Sanket insisted.

“I understand, but please just give us a little more time,” Jia said, her voice pleading. “I will make sure Gaurav finds it and calls you back.”

After a moment of hesitation, Sanket finally agreed to wait a little longer. “Okay, I’ll give you till tomorrow. But please call me back as soon as you guys are ready.”

“I will, I promise,” Jia said before hanging up the phone.

When Jia returned inside, Nandu was curious about the conversation and asked what was going on. Jia avoided the question and instead grabbed the keys to his motorcycle, and asked him to come with her. Nandu protested, saying that he had plans to watch a crucial cricket match with his friends at the local bar, but Jia insisted. She threatened to physically harm him unless he came along.

As Jia and a reluctant Nandu left the house, Gaurav watched from across the road. As soon as they were gone, he retrieved the spare key to the back door and stealthily entered the house.

Gaurav frantically searched through the house, his frustration mounting with each passing moment. He started in the bedroom, where he found Nandu's clothes strewn across the bed and empty beer bottles and torn condom wrappers scattered under it. Swearing under his breath, Gaurav cursed Nandu as his phone started ringing, adding to his irritation. He glared at the unknown number on the screen, muttering in anger.

He switched off the phone and made his way to the kitchen, he couldn't help but notice the stark contrast between the clean space and the mess the bedroom was. Despite the tidiness, Gaurav couldn't find what he was looking for in the kitchen storage.

He moved on to the next room, rummaging through the storage and muttering to himself, "Where could she have put it?" But even there, his search proved fruitless.

Gaurav's hunt for the photo frame seemed never-ending, and he couldn't shake the feeling that Nandu was somehow to blame for its disappearance.

Meanwhile, Jia and Nandu approached Gaurav's house. Nandu couldn't help but ask, "Whose house is this?" He cast a sidelong glance at Jia and added sarcastically, "Oh, right. It's Gaurav's, of course." He chuckled to himself before realisation dawned on him that they were indeed at Gaurav's house.

"Why are we here?" Nandu asked Jia, his brow furrowed in confusion.

Jia turned to him, her expression stern. "Shut up and follow me," she said firmly.

Nandu raised his hands in surrender. "Okay, okay. But how do you know this is Gaurav's house? Have you been here before?"

Jia nodded. "Yes, I used to live here before the wedding. Shh, keep quiet now."

She then tried the door handle, but it was locked. Undeterred, she dug through her purse and retrieved a bunch of keys. With a few deft movements, she managed to unlock the door and Nandu watched in amazement.

“Impressive,” Nandu said, his eyes wide. “You still have the keys.”

Jia rolled her eyes. “Why don’t you be a little useful,” she said,

“Sure, sure... But what are we doing here?” Nandu asked.

“I’m searching for a photo frame,” Jia replied. “Help me find it.”

“Which photo frame?” Nandu asked.

“My wedding photo frame,” Jia said, a hint of frustration creeping into her voice.

“Your wedding photo frame... you don’t need that now,” Nandu said, his brow furrowed in confusion. “You can just buy a new one. Why do you need it now?”

“My brother gave it to me as a gift and I want it back,” Jia explained.

“But...” Nandu began to protest.

“Nandu, search for the frame or your photograph will be stuck on the wall,” Jia threatened, fixing him with a stern gaze. “Now go.”

Nandu reluctantly began searching for the photo frame as Jia looked around the room. As he worked, he couldn't shake the feeling that something was off about all of this.

"What!" Jia exclaimed, noticing Nandu's distraction.

"Nothing," Nandu said, trying to brush it off.

Meanwhile, back at Jia's house, Gaurav went into the bathroom. He opened the cupboard fixed on the wall above and put his hands inside the storage box behind the towels.

Nandu and Jia stood in the empty room of the sparse flat, frustration etched on their faces. Nandu glared at Jia as he gestured to the half-eaten sandwich thrown haphazardly in the open bin. "I've got money riding on my game and friends to meet, but thanks to you and your obsession with that old photo frame, I'm wasting my time here," he complained.

Jia glared back at him, her patience running thin. "Shut up and let me think," she snapped.

But Nandu wasn't finished. "Oh, now I see why you dragged me here. You're spying on your ex-husband. Has he found someone else?"

Jia's anger boiled over as she picked up the kitchen knife and lunged towards Nandu. "I'll kill you and blame it on Gaurav," she spat out, pressing the sharp blade against his neck threateningly. "Want me to do that?"

Nandu quickly backtracked. "No, no, let's search for the frame," he suggested, trying to make peace.

Jia let out a frustrated sigh. "It's not here. Let's go," she said, giving in.

And with that, Nandu and Jia left the house, they're search proving fruitless.

In the bathroom, Gaurav eagerly opened the storage box that he had found, revealing a frame with the wedding photograph. He tore open the brown tape at the back of the frame and took the photograph out. Just as he had hoped, he found the torn 'note' between the white backdrop and the photograph. With a triumphant exclamation, he pocketed the 'note', his pulse racing. Quickly, he put the frame back into the storage box and placed it behind the towels. His excitement turned to nervousness as he overheard Nandu's approaching bike. "Shit, they must be back," he muttered to himself.

As Gaurav overheard Jia and Nandu open the door, he quietly came out of the bathroom. However, he quickly realised that Jia was heading straight towards him, so he entered the bathroom again and hastily hid behind the curtain. Jia entered the bathroom and closed the door behind her. She pulled down her underwear and sat on the toilet to relieve herself. Gaurav became increasingly anxious as he watched from his hiding spot.

After relieving herself, as Jia got up to wash her hands, an uneasy feeling crept through her gut, as if someone was watching. She turned and noticed a towel sticking out of the cupboard. She approached it with a nervous look on her face, her heart racing as she reached for the cupboard handle. Gaurav closed his eyes, hoping to avoid detection, but he couldn't help but peek as Jia opened the cupboard and took out the towel. She then began to undress, and Gaurav couldn't resist the urge to stare at his beautiful wife, feeling embarrassed and guilty for his voyeuristic behaviour. He turned away and closed his eyes again, his heart pounding as he tried to regain control of his emotions. But as Jia turned on the shower, he couldn't resist the temptation to look again, his body flushed with desire. He went red and closed his eyes once more, trying to push down the surging feelings that threatened to overwhelm him. After finishing her shower, Jia wrapped the towel around herself and exited the bathroom, leaving Gaurav to struggle with his emotions.

He composed himself, breathed a sigh of relief and tip-toed out of the bathroom. He quietly exited through the back door as Nandu whistled and complimented Jia on her appearance, stating that she looked as fresh as a lily after the shower. He tried to hug Jia, but she scolded him for his intentions and pushed him away. Nandu playfully responded with an "aww."

Chapter 4

The Deal

The Angadia system in Mumbai is a parallel financial world, mostly operated by Gujaratis, Marwaris and the *Mian bhais*, who help transfer large amounts of money, gold, and diamonds for the jewellery community. The back alleys off Mohammed Ali Road, Kalbadevi and Bhuleshwar in the city and Malad-East in the suburbs effectively serve 70% of their clientele. Madhav *bhai* was known to prefer the suburban angadias for his deliveries, which is what had brought Gaurav to Malad.

As he had in the past, Gaurav circled the Maheshwari lodge house and entered the lane from the back. He knew that Sanket liked to eat Vada pav from the street stall there, so he searched for the vendor and finally located him opposite the Kanha temple.

Gaurav approached the vendor and ordered a Vada pav. "Do you know where Sanket is? Sanket Patel," he asked.

"Patel... wasn't he arrested?" the vendor replied.

"Yes," Gaurav confirmed.

"Then he must be still there, haven't seen him for a while now," the vendor said.

But Gaurav shook his head. "No, he got bail."

As the vendor handed Gaurav the Vada pav, he shrugged. "Then you'll have to look for him inside the market."

Biting into his Vada pav, Gaurav pulled out his phone and called his old colleague, Randhir, at Madhav's place. "Hello, Randhir. It's Gaurav," he said.

"Yes, Gaurav," Randhir replied.

"Do you have any information about Sanket?" Gaurav asked.

"I don't know anything about him, Gaurav. I'm not in that business anymore," Randhir said.

Gaurav hung up the phone, muttering that everyone was useless. Glancing at the tea shop next to the Mandir, he then called Shantanu and invited him to join him for tea.

"Where did Sanket suddenly disappear to?" Gaurav asked Shantanu as they sipped their tea.

"Who knows? I'm also worried," Shantanu replied.

"What do you mean?" Gaurav asked.

"I gave him two bags before the raid. I also need to get my payment, two crores. How much does he owe you?" Shantanu asked.

"My situation is a little different," Gaurav said. "Hey, tell me something, do you still have that guy of yours in the police station?"

"Who? Tambe?" Shantanu replied.

"He'll know. Ask him," Gaurav suggested. "If we can find out anything about Sanket, it will be great."

"He'll ask for money though," Shantanu said, taking out his phone.

A few moments later, Tambe arrived and was introduced to Gaurav.

"What's up, Shantanu? *Tu mala ithe chaha ghyayala bolavalesa? Bola?*" Tambe asked.

"No, Tambe *sahab*, we wanted to ask you about Sanket," Gaurav said.

"That Patel Angadia?" Tambe asked.

"Yes," Shantanu replied.

"Didin't, he get bail?" Tambe asked.

"No idea, you know better *sahab*," Shantanu replied.

"Do you know where he went?" Gaurav asked.

"How much are you looking to get from him?" Tambe asked.

"It's not about the money, Sahab. He's an old friend. That's why," Gaurav explained.

Tambe smirked. "*To juna mitra nahi re.*"

Gaurav gestured for Shantanu to give Tambe some money, which Shantanu did discreetly. "If you find out anything, let us know," Gaurav said.

"Okay," Tambe promised and then left.

Shantanu finished his tea and prepared to leave, reminding Gaurav that he still owed him 500 rupees for the money he had paid Tambe. Gaurav complained about his frugality, and Shantanu jokingly replied that the raids had taught him the value of money. He asked Gaurav how his "*Masterchef*" wife Jia was doing, and Gaurav ranted about Nandu causing their breakup.

"I'm fine, now Nandu is the rockstar for the MasterChef. He's a one-hit-wonder on YouTube, going viral with a single video, and now he's teaching Jia the value of money. After the raids and Madhav *bhai's* death, I went broke and Nandu played his cards well. I got thrown out of the house," Gaurav complained.

Shantanu laughed and said, "Now you're just jealous. Trust me life is much better without a commitment" As Shantanu left, Gaurav began to consider his next move.

He decided the best way was to confront Jia head-on. He arrived at her house and saw her putting out the garbage. He looked for Nandu but didn't see his bike anywhere. Just to be sure, Gaurav called Nandu's phone. He could hear the sound of traffic in the background. Pretending to be a marketing call agent, Gaurav said, "Hello Sir, this is Shershah from Lotta Luck. Your number has been selected for a chance to win rupees one crore. All you have to do is confirm your account..." Nandu cursed and hung up the phone. Gaurav breathed a sigh of relief and headed towards the house.

A surprised Jia opened the door as he rang the bell. She looked around for Nandu and then asked him, "What do you want?"

"Oh, I was worried about you. What's going on? You sounded so frustrated on the phone?" Gaurav replied.

"Come to the point. What do you want?" Jia asked impatiently.

"What do I want? You always get angry so quickly. But I know what you want," Gaurav said with a wink.

"Shut up and leave. I have no interest in you or what you think I want," Jia snapped.

"Okay, let me come to the point. I found the '*note*' that Sanket has been calling you about, on my phone number," Gaurav said.

"What note? Which '*note*' are you talking about?" Jia asked.

"The same one that Sanket has been calling you about. Do you want it or should I leave?" Gaurav said.

"Fine. Give it to me and leave," Jia said.

"Sure, but I have one condition," Gaurav said, winking at her. "I want to spend some time with you."

Jia burst out laughing. "Oh, you are so funny. I think you need to see yourself out, have you forgotten that you were thrown out?"

"I can show myself out, but right now I think you need me to be here. My beloved wife," Gaurav said with a grin.

"Uh huh," Jia said, rolling her eyes.

"Listen, I have a simple idea. We take the money and split it equally. 50-50," Gaurav said.

"Split it? 50-50?" Jia repeated.

"Yes, 50-50, It's not a bad deal," Gaurav said.

"80-20!" Jia offered.

"50-50!" Gaurav countered.

After taking her time to think, Jia offered again, "70-30!"

Gaurav smirked and replied, "50..."

Jia snorted in anger, pushed him out and shut the door in his face. "You know what. I don't want to do any deal with you. Keep your '*note*'. I'll tell Sanket I lost it."

Gaurav followed her through the window. "Hey, I was just joking. You know I'll find Sanket ultimately, but I want to still spend the rest of my life with you. 50-50 is not a bad deal."

Jia didn't fall for Gaurav's charms and went inside. Gaurav waited for a while, but when he realised that Jia wasn't going to open the door, he decided to leave. As he turned to walk towards the gate, he heard Jia call out to him.

"Wait. Come inside."

As Jia and Gaurav kissed passionately, Gaurav tried to undress her. But Jia pushed him away, narrowing her eyes determinedly. "First the '*note*', Gaurav?" she demanded.

Gaurav stared at her for a moment, frustration radiating off of him. Then, with a grumble, he pulled out his phone and showed her a photograph of the note. "See for yourself," he said gruffly.

Jia wasn't convinced. "Don't try to pull a fast one on me, Gaurav," she said, shaking her head in disgust. "You must be out of your mind if you think you can fool me with this."

Gaurav let out a heavy sigh. "Come on, Jia. Just take a look at the date on the photo. It's from today. Listen, I'll call Sanket and we can collect the money. And let's forget all this Nandu nonsense. We are still husband and wife, remember? Whatever is mine is yours. All your past mistakes are forgiven."

"My mistakes are forgiven? Out... get out of here" Jia retorted.

"My mistakes, yaar, please forgive my mistakes," Gaurav backed off. "But please think for a moment, I'm not bluffing," he continued.

Jia hesitated before picking up her phone and dialling Sanket's number. "Sanket *bhai*, we found the '*note*'," she said into the phone.

Gaurav couldn't resist trying to take control of the situation. He snatched the phone from Jia's hand. "Sanket *bhai*, it's Gaurav. *Kem cho*?" he asked, using a casual greeting.

Sanket's voice could be heard on the other end of the line. "*Maja ma...* For a moment I thought you and madam had separated?"

Gaurav chuckled nervously. "Oh, well, you know how many frauds calls we've been getting lately. That's why I was being careful."

Sanket replied, "Well, it's a good thing madam recognised my voice. Otherwise..."

Gaurav cut him off. "Sanket *bhai*, can you tell me where to come? Please give me the address?"

Jia grabbed the phone back from him, her eyes blazing with anger and passion. "Sanket *bhai*, share the location on this number only. And make sure to give the parcel only if both of us are together," she said before hanging up.

She turned to Gaurav and said, "Don't try to take charge, Gaurav. Go on, I'll call and tell you where to meet."

Gaurav tried to kiss Jia again, his lips hungry for hers. But she pushed him away, her body trembling with desire and frustration. "Keep your hands off me, Gaurav. I have to make sure Nandu doesn't cause any more problems."

Their conversation was interrupted by the sound of the door opening. Nandu walked in and stopped in his tracks when he saw Gaurav there, half undressed. He looked at him and then his gaze fell on Jia's crumpled top, he lunged at Gaurav. "What are you doing here?" he yelled.

Gaurav held up his hands in defence. "Hey, calm down. This is my house, remember? And you're just an unwanted guest."

The two men began fighting as Jia tried to intervene. "Stop it, both of you!" she yelled. "Gaurav... leave, Nandu, stop this at once."

Nandu turned to Jia, panting and sweating. "You chose him over me, didn't you? First, you throw out your husband for me, and now you're throwing me out for him. Has he become rich again?"

Jia glared at him. "That's none of your business, and don't talk about taking care of me as your '*wife*'. You're just our neighbour, don't forget that."

A stunned Nandu muttered "*Just our neighbour?*" He lunged for Gaurav but Jia stopped him in his tracks and pushed him out of the house. "Out... I said... leave."

Chapter 5

Nandu

Nandu was born and raised in Goa. He was a member of the influential Dias family, which controlled more than 50% of the fishing business along the Goa coast and had interests in the casino industry. As a child, Nandu was captivated by the carefree lifestyle of the musicians who performed at events and casinos. He dreamed of starting his band and eventually became the lead vocalist and keyboard programmer for his band 'Goa Breeze'.

He was an attractive man – shiny brown-skin, freckled face, tall, and handsome - with a ponytail and was failrly popular with the opposite sex. His band was constantly busy with gigs, and thanks to the Dias name, success came easily for Nandu. However, things took a turn for the worse when he became addicted to alcohol and then hash.

During a Christmas celebration, the NCB (Narcotics Crime Bureau) raided the ship where Nandu and his band were performing a gig. The raid resulted in a shootout, during which several patrons were injured and a constable was tragically killed. Everyone on board was arrested, and Nandu was found to be high on drugs. It was only through his father's influence that he was released from police custody. Admonished for his reckless behaviour and lavish lifestyle, he was sent to rehab and then to Mumbai, where his father had a house in suburban Chembur. In Mumbai, with the help of his old friends, he managed to find work and began writing music for television commercials while also performing online gigs.

When Jia moved in with Gaurav, their neighbour Nandu became infatuated with her. Whenever Gaurav wasn't home, Nandu tried to impress Jia by showering her with compliments and making inappropriate advances. He often told her how lucky Gaurav was to have her and how he wished he were in Gaurav's place.

One day, Nandu walked into Jia's kitchen while Gaurav was at work.

"Hey that's my song 'Angadaiyan' playing on your FM, it has just surpassed 5 million hits. I'm a viral sensation, woohoo!" Nandu said overhearing the song playing in the background. "You look beautiful as always," he continued, leering at her.

Jia politely congratulated him but pushed back on his advances. "That is impressive, Nandu. Thanks for the compliment, but please stop hitting on me. I'm happily married," Jia replied, trying to hide her irritation.

"Come on, Jia. You can do so much better than Gaurav. He doesn't deserve a woman like you," Nandu said, taking a step closer to Jia. "I'm composing a new song just for you," he said, winking at her. "Tu meri Jaanu Hai, I think it could be really special between us."

"I love Gaurav and I'm not interested in you, Nandu. Please leave," Jia said firmly, pushing him away and fed up with Nandu's flirtatious behaviour.

As the months passed, Gaurav began to struggle financially, constantly arguing with Jia. On several occasions, he would storm out of the house in frustration. Nandu saw an opportunity to try and sow discord between the couple.

Tentatively, he approached Jia again, offering her a shoulder to lean on and suggesting he could help promote and grow her business. "I think you're beautiful and intelligent," he told her sincerely. "I have a lot of respect for you. I would love to support you in promoting your cloud kitchen. You won't have to spend anything on it. I hope you'll give me a chance to show you what a good guy I can be."

Jia thanked him politely for his kind words but made it clear that she was not interested in his sympathetic advances.

Nandu knew Gaurav's situation wasn't going to improve anytime soon, and he couldn't help feeling hopeful that

Gaurav would make a mistake soon. His relationship with Jia was hanging by a thread and Nandu knew all he had to do was wait patiently for the right moment to make his move.

He was also aware of Gaurav's habit of assisting his sister-in-law, Kala. So, when he saw Kala arrive on the same morning that Jia had given Gaurav money to buy a bike and set up a delivery service for their kitchen, he saw his opportunity. Eagerly, he crept out of his house and stealthily moved closer to Gaurav's door in an attempt to overhear their conversation.

"Gaurav, I need your help. I don't know who else to turn to," Kala said, her voice shaking with emotion.

"Of course, Bhabhi. Anything I can do to help," Gaurav replied, placing a comforting hand on her shoulder.

"It's Seema. She's gotten into some serious trouble in Bangalore. She was caught shoplifting at Shoppers Stop and now she's facing criminal charges. But it's not her fault - her boyfriend Kumbakaran, the son of a powerful politician, had persuaded her to carry a Rolex for him that he had actually shoplifted and now he's trying to make her take the fall. I need to pay for a lawyer to represent Seema and make sure she doesn't get unfairly punished for something she didn't do," Kala said, tears welling up in her eyes.

"Don't worry, Bhabhi. I'll lend you the money. I know how important it is to get Seema the legal representation she needs to ensure a fair trial," Gaurav said, handing over the bike money to Kala. generously.

"I'll pay you back as soon as I can. I promise," Kala said, gratefully accepting the money.

"Don't worry about it. Just take care of Seema and your family," Gaurav said, giving Kala a reassuring pat on the back.

As Nandu smiled, he heard an auto rickshaw approaching. Carefully, he slipped back into his house. Peering through the crack in the door, he watched as Jia picked up her groceries, got out of the auto-rickshaw and entered the house. A few moments later, he followed her to the door and listened as they spoke.

"Hello Bhabhi, how are you? What's going on?" Jia asked closing the door behind her, noticing the tension in the room.

"Nothing, Bhabhi just needed some help with something," Gaurav said, trying to downplay the situation.

"I see. Well, I hope everything works out for you, Bhabhi. I was going to call you anyway. Gaurav is setting up the delivery service for the kitchen, and we're buying a bike today. I wanted you to do the pooja," Jia said, giving her a sympathetic smile.

Kala looked at Gaurav and realised what Gaurav had done. However, before she could react, Gaurav nodded at her and asked her to leave.

Nandu saw his opportunity and knew that a gentle push could now turn Jia against Gaurav.

That afternoon, when Gaurav was not at home, Nandu approached Jia and told her about Gaurav's generosity towards Kala, even in times of Jia's difficulty. "I'm sorry, Jia, I misjudged your love for Gaurav," Nandu said cautiously. Jia looked at him suspiciously, wondering what new excuse Nandu would use now to try and hit on her again.

"I overheard Kala and Gaurav talking. He gave her the money you had given him for the bike, even though you guys are struggling financially. I admire both of you for your generosity," Nandu continued.

Jia was shocked. "What? How could he do this to me? I trusted him, and he didn't tell me when I met both of them this morning. Going behind my back to help Kala?"

Nandu apologised and tried to fan the flames of her anger towards Gaurav. "I'm sorry you didn't know about it. I thought you knew; I saw you seeing off Kala in the afternoon. It was for Seema's bail; she was caught shoplifting in Bangalore. But still, I can understand how you must feel betrayed by Gaurav's actions."

Jia's eyes blazed as she muttered to herself, "He gave away the money for a bloody thief..."

After Nandu's inflammatory conversation with her, Jia confronted Gaurav and threw him out of the house in a fit of anger. Nandu saw this as his opportunity to make his move on Jia. He had always been infatuated with her and as he watched Jia storm back into the house, he couldn't help but think that she was now his for the taking.

There was another pressing reason why Nandu was so eager to get rid of Gaurav - He knew Jia was gullible when it came to her business but he could take advantage of that only when she was alone. Gaurav knew of his habits and would have seen through his ruse easily. He owed a large sum of money to a drug dealer for a stash of drugs he had purchased and was aware that he couldn't pay off the debt with his current income. Desperate to find a way out, he approached Jia with a proposal after her separation from Gaurav. "I know you're always looking for ways to grow your kitchen and take it to the next level," he said. "Have you ever considered taking out a business loan? I've done some research, and I think it could be a great way to get the financing you need to expand your operations and increase your profits."

Jia was hesitant, but Nandu was persuasive and painted a convincing picture of how a loan could help her achieve her goals. Eventually, she agreed to take out a business loan, trusting Nandu and believing that he had her best interests at heart. However, she was unaware that Nandu had ulterior motives. He introduced her to Junaid, who agreed to provide a business loan at a low-interest rate.

As soon as the loan money came through, Nandu suggested that Jia invest a large sum in an additional kitchen at a garage in Dadar. He said that being close to the busy railway station would help speed up her deliveries and she could expand her reach to new localities. In reality, Nandu used the money to pay off his debt to Junaid.

Jia began to suspect something was wrong when Nandu acted oddly and avoided her questions about the new kitchen at the garage. She confronted him and demanded to know what was going on. Nandu admitted that he had used the money to pay off his debt to Junaid, who was a drug dealer and owned the garage and in reality, there was no kitchen to be rented.

Jia was shocked and angry that Nandu had used her and lied to her. "How could you do this to me?" she yelled. "I trusted you, and you used me to pay off your debt? I can't believe it!"

Nandu knew he had made a mistake and promised to fix it. "I'm sorry, Jia," he said. "I didn't mean to hurt you. I'll do whatever it takes to make this right. Just tell me what you want me to do now." Jia demanded that Nandu clean up the mess and get her money back without involving her. She threw him out of her house and told him she never wanted to see him again.

But things took a turn for the worse when Junaid realised that Nandu had played him and taken a loan in Jia's name to pay off his debt.

Nandu knew he had to meet with Junaid and try to reason with him. He hoped that he could persuade Junaid to accept some other form of payment, or at least give them more time to come up with the money. So, he nervously made his way to Junaid's garage in Dadar.

As soon as he saw Junaid, he knew things weren't going to go well. Junaid was welding a mudguard as Nandu approached. Everyone in the garage stopped working and glared at Nandu.

"Nandu," Junaid said, his voice dripping with contempt. "I'm disappointed in you. I thought we had a deal." He stopped welding.

"We do," Nandu said, his voice shaking. "I just need more time to come up with the money. I promise I'll pay you back, Junaid. Just give me a chance."

Junaid sneered. "I don't think you understand the gravity of your situation," he said. "I'm not some small-time dealer you can just blow off. I don't take kindly to being played."

Nandu swallowed hard, his heart pounding with fear. He knew he was in over his head.

"Please, Junaid," he said. "I'll do anything. Just give me a chance to make things right."

Junaid studied him for a moment, his expression hard and unyielding. Then, he nodded to one of his henchmen, who promptly stepped forward and seized Nandu by the arm and placed it on an iron bar.

Junaid stood up, wielding the welding torch in his hand as he approached a panicking Nandu. He reached forward, bringing the scorching torch close to the tattoo on Nandu's hand, and firmly pressed down on it. Nandu screamed, only to realise that the sparks from the welding torch were smouldering the iron bar on which his hand was pressed. Junaid pressed closer and whispered menacingly in his ear, "Taking a new loan from me to pay back your older loan was a nice idea, but it didn't work."

He could feel the heat radiating from the torch as Junaid added, "You'll do exactly as I say. And if you don't, you'll regret it. I'll make sure of it."

He demanded that Nandu and Jia stay together until Jia's loan was paid off, knowing that Nandu had strong feelings for Jia and believing he could use this to his advantage.

Nandu winced in pain. "What do you want from me?" he asked through gritted teeth.

Junaid sneered. "I want you to stay with Jia and make sure she pays her loan. I know you have strong feelings for her, use them to your advantage." He paused, letting the ultimatum sink in.

Jia was incensed when she discovered Junaid's ultimatum. She couldn't believe that she was being forced to pay a loan that she had been duped into taking, let alone being forced to stay with Nandu against her will. Determined to find a way out of this predicament, Jia set her mind to finding a solution.

Nandu was torn. On the one hand, he desperately wanted to make amends with Jia. But on the other hand, he was terrified of the consequences if he didn't comply with Junaid's demands.

As the days passed, the tension between Nandu and Jia escalated. They were forced to live and work together, and it was clear that Jia resented him, although he still had strong feelings for her. Jia was deeply hurt and angry, and she struggled to find a way to move past the betrayal.

Suddenly, things had taken a dramatic turn with the phone call that day. Jia had been behaving oddly, and then Gaurav had unexpectedly reappeared in her life. Nandu knew that this was not a good sign for him. If Gaurav discovered the loan, there would be consequences. He had previously worked for Madhav *bhai* and had connections that could cause harm to him. Determined not to let his opportunity slip away, Nandu resolved to do whatever it took to protect himself.

So that day, when Jia asked him to leave immediately after he had confronted both of them about what Gaurav was doing in their house, he feigned anger and drove out on his bike, but secretly parked it in the next lane. Circling the society from the back, he returned and waited in the bushes. An Uber arrived and stopped in front of the house. Jia came out of the house, while still speaking on her phone, she got into the Uber, and left. Nandu rushed out of the bushes and immediately got on his bike, starting to tail Jia.

As Nandu followed Jia's Uber through the crowded streets of Mumbai, he couldn't shake the feeling that something was amiss. He knew Jia well enough to know that she wasn't one to just take off without a reason, especially after what had happened earlier in the day. He was even more suspicious when he saw the Uber pull up in front of the Metro cinema at Dhobi Talo. This was odd, Nandu knew that Jia had no reason to be there. He quickly pulled over to the side of the road and watched. Jia got out and hurried inside, still talking on the phone.

Nandu couldn't believe his eyes when he saw Gaurav greet Jia near the box office. He had always known that Jia still had feelings for Gaurav and they had shared a special bond as a married couple, but he had never suspected that they were trying to get back together. He felt a surge of anger and betrayal wash over him as he sat on his bike, watching Jia disappear with Gaurav into the cinema.

He knew he had to do something, but he wasn't sure what. Should he go in and confront Jia? Or should he try to gather more information before making a move? As he sat there, lost in thought, he realised he had no choice but to follow them in.

As Jia and Gaurav sat in the darkened cinema, they could feel Nandu's presence a few rows behind them. They knew that he had followed them, and they knew that they had to get away from him before he found out what they were up to.

As the lights dimmed and the film began, Jia and Gaurav quickly slipped out of their seats and made their way toward the back of the theatre. They knew they had to be careful, hoping that by the time Nandu realised they were gone, it would be too late for him to catch up.

Navigating through the crowded rows of seats, they tried to be as stealthy as possible. When they finally reached the back of the theatre, they slipped out of the back door and into the well-lit parking lot.

As they hurried away, they could hear the interval bell ringing behind them, signalling the break in the film. They knew that Nandu was still inside, unaware that they had escaped.

They made their way through the parking lot and onto the street, trying to blend in with the other passers-by. Just as they thought they were making a clean getaway, they heard Nandu's voice calling out behind them.

"Jia! Gaurav! Where are you guys going?"

They knew they had to act fast. They turned and ran, darting through the crowds. They didn't stop running until they were safely out of sight.

Finally slowing down, they were panting and out of breath. They knew they had to find Sanket quickly. They had a feeling that Nandu wouldn't give up easily, and they had to finish their unfinished business and disappear before he found out.

Chapter 6

Sanket

After making sure that Nandu had not followed them, Jia and Gaurav arrived at Bhuleshwar. Jia took out her phone and called Sanket, "Where do we come, Sanket *bhai*?"

Sanket replied, "I am sending you a location pin; check your phone."

Jia's phone pinged, she looked at it and saw the location map. "Okay," she said.

Sanket continued, "Once you get there, ask anyone for Om Shanti Angadia. I'll be there soon."

Jia and Gaurav followed Sanket's directions and arrived at the old Angadia Street. They entered the Om Shanti Angadia shop, where the angadia looked at them with a questioning expression.

Gaurav told the man that they had been sent by Sanket to pick up a parcel.

"Payment?" the man at the shop asked.

Gaurav handed over half of the coveted '*note*' to the man, who placed it in the glass enclosure. The man then picked up the phone and called Sanket.

"*Kem chho, Sanket bhai, Ravi aa hu. Payment karva ma aa chhu,*" the man at the shop said. "*Hae, theek aa, main tumari aave chhe balance levaar par wait karva rahya hu.*"

After hanging up the phone, Ravi turned towards Jia and Gaurav. "Sanket *bhai* is coming with the balance payment. I'll give you your parcel then. Would you like some tea while you wait?"

"No," Jia retorted, while Gaurav said, "Yes."

Jia exchanged angry glances with Gaurav as they waited for Sanket to arrive.

Meanwhile, Nandu emerged from the Hussaini mosque onto the by-lanes, his eyes frantically scanning the street for Jia and Gaurav but coming up empty. As he walked down the street, he crossed paths with Sanket, who was engrossed in a phone conversation with the angadia at the Om Shanti Angadia shop. "*Thika che, avisa, avisa...*" Sanket said before hanging up.

Without warning, a car careened across the road, scraping Nandu and crashing into Sanket with a sickening thud. The impact sent Sanket flying, and he lay unconscious on the ground as the bystanders rushed to help him. Nandu, overwhelmed by the sudden turn of events, could only stare in horror as a stabbing pain numbed his hand.

A honking bike jolted him out of his stupor, and he scrambled to his feet, rushing over to Sanket's side. He could hear the crowd murmuring around him, "He's dead." The realisation that it could have been him sent a chill down Nandu's spine, and he struggled to shake off the sense of danger that seemed to be closing in on him.

Soon, an ambulance and the police arrived on the scene. Constable Tambe looked around and asked the bystanders, "Is there a witness to the accident?"

"Sir, him," said a lady, pointing at Nandu. "The car hit him first, but poor thing, the other man died saving him."

Nandu's mind was racing as Tambe approached him and asked for his account of the incident. "*Aye, Tujhe nava kaya*?"

"N-Nandu," Nandu stammered, still in shock.

Sanket's body was carefully loaded into the ambulance and taken away, and Nandu watched in a daze as it drove off. Patil noticed that Nandu was wincing in pain and asked, "Are you hurt?"

"No, no, it's just a scratch; I'm just glad I am still alive," Nandu said, looking down at his scratched hand.

Back at the Om Shanti Angadia, Ravi received a call and his expression changed to one of horror. "*Kya hua?*" he asked the caller. He listened for a moment before hanging up and turning to Jia and Gaurav. "Sanket has been hit by a car," Ravi continued "It's serious. They've taken him to Cama Hospital."

Jia and Gaurav looked at each other in shock. Ravi looked at Jia and said, "You should go to the hospital right away. Bring the balance payment from Sanket, and I'll give you the parcel. Here, keep this with you." He handed the torn '*note*' back to Jia.

Jia and Gaurav looked at each other, panic written on their faces. Both of them ran out of the shop frantically.

Jia and Gaurav arrived at the Cama hospital, which was overcrowded with patients, as is typical of government hospitals. The line for the enquiry desk was long and slow. Gaurav looked around and stopped a nurse who was walking past them. "Excuse me, where is the emergency room?" he asked.

The nurse replied, "It's straight ahead, at the end of the corridor on the left."

Jia and Gaurav rushed down the corridor towards the emergency room, not realising that they had passed the OPD (outpatient department) room where Nandu was receiving first aid for his injury. Unbeknownst to all of them, destiny had brought the three of them back together. When Jia and Gaurav reached the emergency room, they saw Tambe sitting outside the door.

"Shit," Gaurav remarked.

"What happened?" Jia asked.

"Tambe," Gaurav said, pointing towards the constable. "He knows me."

Jia looked at Gaurav and, motioning to him, turned to go and ask Tambe about Sanket. However, Gaurav pulled her behind a pillar.

"What are you doing?" Jia asked.

"Shh," Gaurav said, pointing down the corridor. "Look, it's Nandu."

Jia was shocked to see Nandu there. She exclaimed," How did he get here? Do you think he knows about Om Shanti? Did he follow us here from there?"

"I don't think so, looks like a coincidence, otherwise he would have confronted us at Om Shanti itself"

They moved closer to overhear Nandu and Tambe's talk.

As Nandu approached Tambe, looking worried, Tambe asked, *"Ey shaney, tujya kya lagta hai, accident kaise hua?"*

Nandu hesitated before explaining, "We were all coming out of the cinema when the accident happened. I was crossing the road and a car came at me at high speed. I tried to move out of the way, but it hit me on the side and I fell. When I got up, I realised that the driver had hit someone else as well." He looked at Tambe with concern in his eyes. "Did he die?"

Tambe nodded gravely. "Yes, he did."

Nandu's face fell and he crossed his hand and made a cross sign "Oh no. Thank God I am alive," he said, looking down at his scratched hand.

Jia and Gaurav, who had been watching from a distance, overheard the conversation. Jia whispered, "What do we do now?"

Gaurav watched as Nandu signed a document and left. Tambe told him, "I'll call if I need you again. Okay?"

Nandu nodded his head and headed out of the corridor. Jia and Gaurav stepped behind the pillar as he passed them. Gaurav looked at Jia and then towards the emergency room. He saw a nurse come out of the room. Both of them approached her and asked, "Excuse me, can you tell us what happened to the person who was brought in here?"

The nurse hesitated before saying, "I'm sorry, but the person died in the accident. Was he your relative?"

Jia nodded. The nurse continued, "The police are waiting for the post-mortem report. You can check with Tambe, he brought the body in, and he will know when they will release the body."

Gaurav nodded, thanking the nurse before turning to Jia and saying, "You should go talk to Tambe and confirm that it's Sanket." He pulled out his phone and showed her an old photo of Sanket from the gallery.

As Jia walked towards Tambe, she couldn't help but wonder how Sanket's death would affect their chances of retrieving the parcel. God knew she needed whatever money she could get to escape from Nandu and Junaid's clutches.

Jia approached Tambe, panting and out of breath. "I received a call saying that my husband had been in an accident," she said, her voice shaking with emotion.

Tambe raised an eyebrow and looked at her intently. "*Aahe tu kon asto*?"

"I just told you, I'm his wife," Jia replied, her voice dripping with sarcasm. "I received a call saying that my husband had been in an accident."

"I've never seen you before. He was in jail for two years and you did not visit him even once?" Tambe pointed out.

"He told me not to come," Jia said, her voice laced with sadness. She looked at him and said sarcastically, "Now I understand why he didn't want me to come."

Tambe took out his notebook. "And what's your name?"

"*Sulbha*," Jia said.

"*Sulbha* what? *Patel*?" Tambe asked.

A silent Jia glared at him with anger.

"For the records, *Sulbhaben*," Tambe replied.

Tambe led Jia into the room where Sanket's body was lying and asked her to identify it. Jia identified Sanket's body, tears streaming down her face. "*Hae Sanket aahe. Tame kyu jaldi chali gayo*, Sanket?" she sobbed.

Tambe watched her silently, his expression turned sceptical. "Drama," he muttered to himself.

Jia noticed that Sanket was not wearing a watch and she could not see his phone anywhere. A few of his blood-soaked belongings were kept on a side table next to the stretcher. She turned to Tambe and asked, "Where are all his things? His watch? His phone?"

Tambe raised an eyebrow. "Everything is being inventoried by the nurse. We still have to do the post-mortem," he said.

Jia asked, "When will I get everything back? When will the post-mortem be done?"

Tambe replied, "It'll take about two to three days. After the post-mortem, his belongings will be deposited at the police station. I'll call you when everything is done, you can come then and collect everything. The body will be released from the hospital mortuary post that"

Jia gave a quick look around before following Tambe out of the room.

Outside the room, in the corridor, Tambe spotted a chaiwallah walking past. He stopped him immediately and picked up a cup. "Chai?" he asked, looking at Jia. She shook her head and moved quietly towards the pillar where Gaurav was standing, leaving Tambe engaged with the chaiwallah.

Gaurav looked at Jia, concern etched on his face. "What happened?" he asked.

Jia's voice was laced with tension as she replied. "It's Sanket. He's dead."

Gaurav's expression hardened. "Did you check his pockets? Did you find anything?" he said, his voice dripping with suspicion.

Jia sighed. "Gaurav, he's dead. I could only stare at his dead body. Tambe was standing right behind me," she said, her voice laced with irritation.

Gaurav nodded. "Do me a favour, please take Tambe aside. I'll see what I can do," he said, his voice low and determined. Jia nodded and walked towards Tambe.

She called out to him, as he was about to pay the chaiwallah. She stopped him and took some money out of her purse, giving it to the chaiwallah. Gaurav took advantage of the moment and disappeared into the emergency room. Jia and Tambe stood in uncomfortable silence, the tension between them growing with each passing moment. Tambe smiled at Jia and sipped his tea.

Gaurav stealthily entered the room, his heart racing with fear and anxiety. He frantically searched Sanket's body, muttering to himself about the lengths people go to for money. "Sorry, Sanket *bhai*," he whispered, feeling guilty for what he was about to do.

But as he rummaged through Sanket's pockets and wallet, he couldn't find the '*note*' he was looking for. He frantically pawed through the bloodstained clothes, hoping to find some clue, but to no avail.

Just as Gaurav was about to give up and leave, he spotted Nandu approaching Jia and Tambe through the crack in the door. His heart skipped a beat as he quickly closed the door, leaving just a small opening to peek through. He watched with bated breath as the scene unfolded, his mind racing with fear and uncertainty.

Nandu had returned to the hospital and was surprised to see Jia talking to Tambe as he walked in. He confronted her, asking what she was doing there. Tambe inquired about their relationship, and Jia explained that Nandu was her neighbour. Tambe seemed a bit suspicious and looked quizzically at Nandu, he asked, "*Tumhi apanar neighbour-cha pati pahile nahi ghetla*?"

Nandu retorted, "Her husband?"

Jia quickly stopped Nandu mid-sentence and said, "He is my neighbour from Ahmedabad, my hometown, and he doesn't know my husband." She then winked at Nandu and asked him to leave. "Nandu, when did you come to Mumbai? You never called? What a coincidence! Please don't tell my mom about the accident. She will be stressed. I will tell her myself."

A confused Nandu looked at her suspiciously before turning to walk away.

Gaurav continued to observe them from the emergency room as Nandu stopped after taking a few steps and turned back. Tambe asked him why he had returned, and Nandu rummaged in his pockets before handing him a scout bag and a broken phone.

"So, you found this scout bag on your neighbour who was in the accident?" Tambe asked.

Nandu irritated. "He was not my neighbour and yeah, he was using this phone when the accident happened and had this bag in his other hand. I had forgotten to give it back earlier."

Tambe looked sceptical. "And you didn't take anything out from it?"

"No, I didn't," Nandu insisted. "I'm not a thief, Sahab. I wouldn't have come back if I did, would I?"

Jia was shocked when she saw the scout bag. Tambe then headed towards the emergency room, asking Jia to follow him "*Aaoo Sulbhaben...*" and telling Nandu to stay put "*aye tu yaha ruk.*"

A confused Nandu muttered under his breath "*Ahmedabad... Sulbhaben...*" he saw both of them enter the room and quietly stepped in behind them.

Gaurav watched nervously as they all walked towards the room. He frantically scanned the room, searching for a place to hide. But it was too late. The door opened and Tambe, Jia, and Nandu entered.

Nandu's heart raced as he saw Sanket's body lying on the stretcher, surrounded by his personal belongings on a nearby table. Tambe placed the phone and scout bag with the rest of the belongings before turning to leave with Jia and Nandu. Nandu cast a suspicious glance at the body before pointing at it and looking at Jia.

"This is not...," Nandu began, but Jia cut him off with a glare.

"So, you didn't know her husband, *tumchya aai zhali* wedding *madhe* attend *keli aahe ka*?" Tambe said as he motioned them to follow him out.

As the three left the room, Gaurav breathed a sigh of relief. He had climbed out of the window in the room and witnessed everything, clinging to the drainage pipe next to it. He climbed back into the room through the window.

He went to the table and rummaged through Sanket's scout bag that Tambe had just left along with the other belongings, but he found no torn '*note*' or money in it. Disappointed, Gaurav picked up the phone and was relieved to find that it was still working. He placed the phone in front of Sanket's face and unlocked it with his face ID, quickly deleting the call records to avoid any suspicion of his calls to Jia's phone.

Tambe, Jia, and Nandu emerged from the emergency room, to be greeted by SI Patil, Tambe's senior. Tambe saluted him and said, "Jai hind Sahab!"

"What happened?" he asked.

"Sir, there has been an accident," Tambe replied, looking grave.

SI Patil looked sceptical. "Any death?" he inquired.

"One, he escaped," Tambe explained, gesturing towards Nandu.

SI Patil sighed heavily.

The group walked towards the emergency room, Gaurav looked at them and ducked under the stretcher. As Tambe and SI Patil entered the room, Gaurav overheard their conversation.

"Has the post-mortem been done yet?" SI Patil asked.

"Sir, we are still waiting for it," Tambe replied.

Jia chimed in, "Tambe Sahab, thank you. I'm going home. Please call me after the post-mortem is finished, and I'll come to pick up the body."

SI Patil turned to Jia and asked, "Who is this?"

"This is the deceased's wife, *Sulbhaben*" Tambe replied.

"Where did you come from?" SI Patil asked Jia sympathetically.

"Ahmedabad," Jia replied, taking hold of Nandu's arm she stepped forward, followed by Tambe and SI Patil.

Gaurav emerged from under the stretcher and walked to the window. He stepped out and, holding onto the drainage pipe, jumped down.

He quickly rushed out of the corridor, following Jia and Nandu as they entered a small tea shop across the road.

Inside the cold and gloomy tea shop, Nandu and Jia were in the midst of an intense argument, their voices echoing off the peeling walls. "What are you doing here?" Nandu demanded, his arms crossed over his chest. "Neighbour... Ahmedabad... care to explain?"

Jia shot him a challenging look. "What are you doing here? You tell me first."

"I... If you have forgotten, I just had an accident and needed first aid. And what about that corpse inside? When did he become your husband?" Nandu asked, his voice dripping with sarcasm.

A waiter approached them. Jia looked at him and ordered two teas.

"And what were you doing with Gaurav? Since when did you start watching movies with him again?"

Nandu countered, his eyes narrowing.

Jia let out a harsh laugh. "You were stalking me, weren't you? I saw you following us everywhere. What do you care anyway? You were always after my money."

Nandu's face turned red with anger, "Stalking? I was burning with jealousy! Tell me the truth, '*Sulbhaben*' or I'll tell Tambe everything," Nandu replied, his voice laced with a threat.

For a moment, Jia just looked at Nandu, her eyes locked with his. And then, without warning, she leaned in and kissed him. Nandu was taken aback, his eyes wide with shock. Jia whispered a threat in his ear.

"Tell him willingly, *darling*, and I'll also disclose where you get your stash and the loan from... Okay, baby..." She said, her voice low and menacing.

With that, she pushed Nandu aside and told him to leave. "Leave... right now," she said, turning her face away.

Gaurav, who had been following them, observed the whole interaction. He saw Nandu leave reluctantly and then waited for a while to make sure Nandu didn't return. Jia took out her phone and called Gaurav, who looked at her incoming call and then approached her.

"Wow... that was brave, but did you have to kiss him?" Gaurav said as he sat down next to Jia.

She glared at him. The waiter brought the tea that had been ordered and placed it in front of them. He was surprised to see Gaurav sitting there instead of Nandu.

Jia asked him if he had found the note. "Did you get the *note*?" she asked.

"No, nothing; There was no money in the bag. And his pockets were also empty," Gaurav replied, a look of defeat on his face.

"I think Nandu took out whatever money was there before giving the scout bag to Tambe," Jia said, a thoughtful expression on her face.

"Why would he do that? I think Tambe may have cleaned out Sanket's pockets earlier in the ambulance itself. Look at how he was talking," Gaurav said, a sceptical look on his face.

Jia thought for a moment. "Let's do one thing. I'll follow Nandu, and you follow Tambe. One of them must have the *note*."

"And if it's with Nandu, you'll join hands with him and take all the money and disappear?" Gaurav said, a hint of anger in his voice.

"What!" Jia exclaimed, her eyes widening in shock.

Gaurav argued,"You threw me out of the house for doing charity and didn't even want to tell me that Sanket had called you in the first place. How am I supposed to trust you?"

Jia exclaimed, "That woman was completely ripping you off! For goodness' sake, her daughter is a shoplifter. You're completely blind when it comes to your relatives. And if you think you can find Sanket's '*note*' without me, go ahead and try. Good luck with that."

Gaurav stared at her. The silence weighed heavily on Jia. She looked at Gaurav and gave in. "Okay, we need each other. Let's get this done together."

Gaurav smiled and finished his tea. "Let's go. Find Nandu."

Jia and Gaurav arrived at Jia's house, looking for Nandu. Gaurav scanned the area, but there was no sign of him anywhere.

"Nandu isn't here," Gaurav said, a look of concern on his face. "I have no idea where he could have gone," Jia replied, her brow furrowed in worry.

Just then, they heard the sound of a motorcycle starting up. They rushed towards the sound and saw Nandu talking on the phone as he rode away. "We have to follow him," Gaurav said, his expression determined. "But how? We don't know where he went?" Jia replied, her voice filled with frustration.

"Wait... Now let me think where could he have gone?" Gaurav said, his expression filled with concern. He closed his eyes and replayed back the scene in his mind. "He was talking to someone on the phone..." he said, his eyes snapping open. "Let's go," he took his phone out "I think I know where he's gone," Gaurav said, his expression determined.

Chapter 7

The Torn Note

The stress of following Jia and Gaurav, coupled with the accident, had taken a toll on Nandu. He needed to get a fix, and quickly. He still didn't know what Jia and Gaurav had been after, or how they were linked to Sanket. But he knew that once his mind relaxed, he would be able to figure it out. He had called Junaid and given him a heads-up. Earlier in the day, he had taken out whatever money he found in Sanket's scout bag, before returning an empty bag to Tambe, and he intended to get what he wanted.

Gaurav and Jia found themselves outside a garage in the narrow street behind Dadar station.

"Wait!" Jia exclaimed. "I've been here before. This is where the new kitchen was supposed to be set up."

Gaurav looked at her quizzically. "New kitchen?" he asked, but his question was interrupted by the sound of Nandu's voice.

The two of them turned and saw Nandu huddled with a man in what appeared to be the cashier's room. They moved closer and listened to the conversation between the two of them.

Gaurav leaned over to Jia and whispered, “That’s Junaid, the drug dealer who supplies Nandu.”

Jia’s expression changed as she put two and two together. “That’s the guy who threatened me,” she said, her voice filled with anger. “Nandu misled me and persuaded me to take a false business loan from him. Turned out, it was all just payment for his old debts with Junaid. When I found out and tried to report him, Junaid beat up Nandu and then threatened me with dire circumstances. Now you know why I needed to find the ‘*note*’ and get whatever money I could and also the reason why I didn’t tell you about Sanket’s call.”

Gaurav looked at Jia with surprise. “Why didn’t you tell me earlier?” he asked.

Jia explained, her voice laced with bitterness. “He lied to me and used me.”

Gaurav nodded, his eyes livid, his expression filled with anger at Nandu. “And I got thrown out for doing charity,” he said. “We have to do something about this.”

Jia nodded in agreement. “We can’t let him get away with this. We have to expose him and make sure he pays for what he's done," she said, her voice filled with determination.

Inside, Nandu was paying off Junaid. "Here, take this. Now give me my *nasha*," Nandu said gruffly, sliding a stack of cash across the table to Junaid.

Junaid opened the drawer and retrieved a small, unmarked sachet, carefully handing it over to Nandu. He motioned Nandu to wait as he started counting the notes that Nandu had just given him.

"Wait... What is this?" Junaid said, holding up a couple of torn notes with a frown.

"Give me clean notes, no torn notes," he demanded sternly.

Jia and Gaurav looked at each other uneasily and then at the *torn notes* lying in front of Junaid.

Nandu frantically searched around in his pocket but came up empty.

"I don't have any. I'll pay the balance next time," Nandu said, his voice filled with desperation.

"No... Now," Junaid replied firmly.

"Come on, I'm a regular customer," Nandu pleaded.

"If you die tomorrow, it'll be my loss. Pay up. Then take it," Junaid said, taking the sachet back from Nandu, his voice laced with threat.

"What the hell! I've been bringing you customers for your fake business loans and also buying and selling stash for you... and you can't trust me with a few grand?" Nandu exclaimed, his eyes widening in disbelief.

"Looks like you have forgotten who you are talking to. You want it, pay for it. Understand?" Junaid said, his voice cold and hard.

"Fine... I'll figure something out," Nandu said, his expression resigned.

Gaurav cautiously pulled out his phone and discreetly signalled for Jia to be silent. He then dialled Shantanu's number and spoke to him in a hushed, urgent tone. "Shanky, I need you to do me a favour. Call Tambe and tell him that there is a drug deal going down at D'Souza's Garage in Chuna Galli, Dadar. After the raid, you can claim the reward they offer for helping locate and expose drug cartels."

As the sound of approaching police sirens grew louder, Junaid frantically took out a bag and put all the powder sachets in it. "Police! We have to leave, now!" he yelled to his boys, his voice urgent.

Without hesitation, he grabbed the bag of drugs and rushed through the back door along with his boys, barely avoiding detection.

When SI Patil and Constable Tambe arrived at the scene with a few other officers, they found the room empty. Patil turned to Tambe with frustration and disappointment. “Tambe, what’s going on here? You’re such a fool! How did you let them get away like this?” he scolded.

Tambe, with shame on his face, mumbled an apology. Just then, one of the constables called out from the back of the room, drawing their attention to the backdoor.

As Jia and Gaurav watched, they saw Inspector Patil, Tambe, and the rest of the constables chase after Junaid and his accomplices. “I think they’ve left,” Jia said, her voice filled with relief.

“Let’s go,” Gaurav urged, standing up.

“Where?” Jia asked.

“Inside, Junaid’s cabin,” Gaurav replied.

The two of them began searching the room for the money, with Gaurav heading towards the drawers. “These are locked,” he said, trying in vain to force them open with a small screwdriver.

Tambe and the constables sprinted after Junaid and his accomplices. Despite their desperate attempts to escape, Tambe was determined to bring them to justice. As they ran, they reached a backdoor that opened onto a narrow street near the station. Tambe noticed a scattering of white powder and several sachets on the ground and saw a druggie sitting nearby, his nose buried in one sachet.

Tambe grabbed the druggie and demanded to know where did he get the sachets from.

"Tell me where did you find these sachets!" Tambe shouted, his eyes blazing with anger.

"S-Sachets, don't know, Sahab," the druggie stammered. "I just found them on the ground. I swear!"

Tambe didn't believe him. He slapped the druggie again, harder this time. "Did you see anyone go from here!"

"Ouch, please don't hurt me!" the druggie cried out with glazed eyes. "I saw a group of men running towards the railway yard and jumping over the fence. One of them dropped their bag, and some sachets fell out when they retrieved it."

Tambe signalled to the constables to follow the trail.

At the railway yard behind the station, Junaid and his gang split up. Junaid tried to shake off Tambe by climbing the narrow bridge connecting the abandoned platform, while the gang members cut through the railway tracks. Anticipating Junaid's move, Tambe raced across the tracks and scrambled up the opposite side. Seeing Tambe closing in, Junaid shouted for help to his gang, who stopped running and engaged in a fierce struggle with Tambe. In the melee, Tambe was wounded, but he refused to let go and finally succeeded in apprehending a couple of the gang members with the help of the other constables.

Back at the garage, Jia watched Gaurav struggling with the screwdriver. She picked up a crowbar and started hitting the drawer determined to help Gaurav open the drawer, but to no avail. As she looked around the cabin for anything else they could use, the sound of Tambe and Patil approaching interrupted her thoughts. "Gaurav, they're back," she said as panic set in on her. Without hesitation, Jia and Gaurav fled the room and took cover.

They watched as Tambe and the constables arrived at the cabin with a couple of Junaid's staff members, Inspector Patil instructed them to bring the bag inside. The staff obeyed, laying the bag on the ground.

Patil then ordered the staff to open the drawer. One of them took out a bunch of keys and unlocked it, revealing nothing inside. Patil looked around the cabin with disappointment while Tambe began slapping and berating the staff.

"*Tyacha maal kuthe ahe? kuthe ahe*?" Patil demanded Where is the rest of the stash? Where is it hidden?" his voice filled with anger.

The staff remained silent, cowering under Tambe's wrath. Patil walked to the glass walls and looked around the room. His eyes landed on the toolboxes in the cupboard. He fiddled with them and then managed to open them, and to his surprise, the stash of illegal goods and a large sum of cash flew out.

"Seize all of this," Patil ordered, as Tambe collected everything and placed it in his custody. Jia and Gaurav looked on helplessly, knowing their chances of getting their hands on the money had now dwindled.

As the police left the cabin with the staff and the stash, Jia and Gaurav followed, feeling defeated. "It looks like we won't be getting anything now," Jia said dejectedly.

"Wait, there's still a chance, I didn't see any *torn notes*," Gaurav said, trying to remain hopeful. "Maybe it is somewhere else, with Junaid or with Nandu."

Little did they know, Nandu had witnessed everything from the shadows. He had overheard Jia and Gaurav talking about the '*torn note*' and, upon searching his own pockets, found three *torn notes* that Junaid had returned to him earlier.

"These lovebirds are searching for the *torn note?* Perhaps today's my lucky day," Nandu thought to himself, a wicked grin spreading across his face. He had the key to both Jia and a ton of cash, or whatever the *torn note* was worth. All he had to do now was to meet Jia alone and confront her, and he knew exactly where he would do that.

Nandu arrived at the police station early the next day, eager to give his statement about the accident he and Sanket had been involved in a couple of days ago. As he walked through the doors, he was greeted by Constable Tambe, who was sporting a bandaged hand. "Hey Sahab," Nandu noticed the injury and asked with genuine concern, "*Kasa aahe tujha hatat? Kuthla kaamat aahe tujhya hatatla*?"

Tambe nodded, wincing slightly at the memory. "Yeah, it was a tough night. One of the suspects put up quite a fight, and I ended up getting hurt in the scuffle. But it was worth it, we managed to arrest a couple of them," he replied.

Nandu nodded in understanding, although he secretly knew that Tambe was referring to the events that had taken place at the garage the previous night. He focused on the task at hand and began answering Tambe's questions about the accident.

Tambe took out his notebook from the drawer under the table and asked. "We have gone through the CCTV footage from around the accident location and are trying to find the person responsible," he said. "Now, did you happen to remember what the driver looked like or the number plate of the truck that hit you?"

Nandu shook his head regretfully. "I'm sorry, but everything happened so fast. I didn't get a good look at the driver or the number plate. All I know is that it was a large truck, possibly a delivery truck," he said.

"What was the colour of the truck? The CCTV footage is black and white" Tambe asked, as he made a note of Nandu's information.

Nandu thought for a moment and said "It was bright yellow... and the front mudguard was damaged from the right"

"Anything else you can remember?" Tambe quipped. Nandu shook his head "No, I was in both shock and pain, I will let you know if I remember anything else."

Tambe thanked Nandu for his time. "We'll do our best to track down the truck based on this information," he said. "Thank you for your cooperation."

Nandu looked at Tambe and asked, "Did you find out who Sanket was? Did you figure out what he did for a living?"

Tambe nodded gravely. "Sanket was an Angadia. He moved money for the local jewellers. We arrested him a couple of years ago for moving black money and sent him to jail, and he had just been released on bail a few days before the accident."

Nandu couldn't believe what he was hearing. He shook his head in disbelief and said, "I had no idea. I'm so sorry to hear that. His death is even more tragic now, imagine he was just released."

Tambe nodded and smirked sarcastically. "Yes, it is a tragic loss and he will be missed by the jewellers." As Nandu stared at him, Tambe looked at him with a poker face and said, "*Tu aata yeu shakto.*"

Nandu took a few steps to leave and then stopped. He turned and asked Constable Tambe about the status of Sanket's post-mortem examination. "Has the post-mortem been completed yet?" he inquired. "*Sulbhaben* wanted to know when to collect his body and belongings."

Tambe raised an eyebrow, becoming suspicious of Nandu's intentions. "Why do you want to know? "*Tu karun jya kalal aahe tari neighbour la mhantat?*" he smirked.

Nandu explained that he just wanted to know when she should be coming to the police station, he was just helping her out with anything she needed. Tambe was not satisfied with Nandu's explanation and told him to leave. "The post-mortem was completed yesterday itself. As for *Sulbhaben*, she will be at the police station any time now to collect Sanket's belongings. We have everything ready for her," he said. "*Tu aata yeu shakto.*"

Their conversation was interrupted when Jia walked into the police station, and Nandu couldn't help but smile at the sight of her. "*Arre Sulbhaben*, how are you? Come, come, I was just enquiring about you from Tambe Sahab," he said, trying to get her attention. Jia was surprised to see Nandu at the police station and Tambe greeted her, "Come, come, *Sulbhaben*, sit down..." Jia replied, "Yes, sir. Thank you."

Tambe informed Jia that the post-mortem had been done and that death by accident had been confirmed. He asked Jia if she had collected the body from the hospital. Tambe handed over Sanket's belongings to Jia, who nervously looked through Sanket's scout bag.

"Tambe Sahab, I had given Sanket some money, but it's not here now," Jia said.

A surprised Tambe, looked at Nandu, "How much money was it?"

"Fifty-thousand rupees and some small change," Jia replied.

"Did you take the money out before you returned the scout bag that day?" Tambe asked Nandu.

"No, sir, I told you that day itself in the hospital. I am an honest man. *Sulbhaben* will vouch for me. If you want, you can check," Nandu replied, turning out his pockets and showing some torn notes with a wink. "Look, I don't even have money on me now, just a few *torn notes*. Where would I hide fifty-thousand rupees?"

Jia nervously looked at the *torn notes* and then at Nandu, realising that he must have seen and overheard everything at the garage. She kicked herself for not looking out for him the previous night before talking.

As Nandu and Jia prepared to leave the police station, Tambe called out to Nandu. "Hey, you, leave those *torn notes* behind. It's illegal to carry them around."

"Don't worry, sir, I will exchange them at the bank," replied Nandu hastily, stuffing the *torn notes* into his pocket with a wiliness that didn't go unnoticed by Jia.

Tambe smiled and asked him to take the *torn notes* out. "No, just leave them with me. *Mi tyaci kalaji gheina.* You don't want to get into any trouble, do you?"

Nandu reluctantly handed over the *torn notes* to Tambe. Jia coughed to contain her smile as Nandu glared at her. He was about to say something when a woman crying loudly entered the police station, drawing Tambe's attention.

He rushed to see what was happening and was shocked to see the woman claim that she had got a call from the hospital that her husband had been involved in an accident and they asked her to go to the police station and meet Constable Tambe. "What happened? Why are you crying?" Tambe asked, trying to calm her down.

"My husband, Sanket," the woman sobbed. "*Koi madad karo. Mane abhi pata chhuka hu. Kripya, tumhne madad karni padegi...*"

Tambe looked at the woman with suspicion. "If you are Sanket's wife, then who is this woman?" he asked, gesturing towards Jia.

The woman looked at Jia and Nandu, and her expression changed from one of grief to one of anger. "She is not his wife, I am" she spat. "She's just pretending to be his wife to get his belongings."

Jia's eyes widened in shock as she realised that she had been found out. "We have to get out of here," she said to Nandu, taking off towards the exit.

Tambe shouted for them to stop, but Jia and Nandu were already out of the door and running down the street. Tambe called out for Constable Gaikwad to follow him and try to catch them "Gaikwad, *pudhil aahe! Unhacha pakadnaar aahe*!"

Outside, Nandu and Jia split up at the junction, each running in a different direction to try to lose Tambe and Gaikwad. Tambe decided to follow Jia, knowing that she was the more likely of the two to have something to hide. He chased her through the crowded streets, dodging people, cars and taxis as he went.

Jia was a fast runner and quickly outpaced the injured Tambe. He struggled to keep up with her, his legs aching and his breath coming in ragged gasps. He could see her darting through the crowds ahead of him, always just out of reach.

Despite his best efforts, Tambe was unable to catch up with Jia. She disappeared into the crowds, leaving him alone and panting in the middle of the street. Dejected, Tambe made his way back to the police station, wondering how Jia and Nandu were connected and if there was more to Sanket's accident.

Back at the police station, Tambe noticed that the woman who had come in crying and claiming to be Sanket's wife had already left. He called out to the other constables, "Where did she go? Did any of you see which way she left?"

The constables shook their heads. "No, sir. She left immediately after you and Gaikwad rushed out to chase those two."

Tambe cursed under his breath and walked over to his desk. He noticed that the *torn notes* that Nandu had given him earlier were also missing. He called out to the constables again, "Has anyone seen the *torn notes* that Nandu gave me? They were on the desk just a few minutes ago."

The constables searched around the table but the notes were nowhere to be found. Tambe shook his head, feeling frustrated and confused. It was clear that something was going on, and he knew he needed to get to the bottom of it. He decided to check the CCTV footage to see if it could provide any clues.

Chapter 8

The Parcel

After escaping from Tambe, Jia had taken a taxi and walked into Churchgate railway station. She had tried to call Gaurav, but his phone had been switched off. She sat at the railway station, trying to figure out what to do next when her phone rang. It was Gaurav.

“Gaurav, what’s going on? Why is your phone switched off?” Jia asked as she answered the call.

“Jia, check the message on your phone,” Gaurav replied urgently.

Jia’s phone pinged with the message tone. She looked at it and saw a location map for Malad-East. She immediately got on to a local train and headed to Malad.

Upon arriving at the Malad station, Jia followed the map and soon found herself outside a deserted building on a narrow street. The sound of bells from the temple next door punctuated the air. She looked around, wondering where to go when her phone pinged again. It was another message from Gaurav, asking her to come to the third floor of Mehta House, the building opposite the temple.

Jia cautiously made her way up the stairs, keeping an eye out for any suspicious activity. When she reached the third floor, she saw a door slightly ajar and could hear faint voices coming from inside. She slowly pushed the door open and peered inside.

Inside, Jia saw Gaurav sitting at a table with Ravi from Om Shanti Angadia and the woman who had come crying into the police station as Sanket's wife. Gaurav looked up as she entered and motioned her to quietly close the door behind her.

"Jia, I'm so glad you are safe," Gaurav said as he hugged Jia.

"Gaurav, what's going on? What is she doing here?" Jia asked, pointing towards the woman, who smiled.

Gaurav explained the situation to Jia. "I saw what was happening at the police station. When Tambe asked Nandu to hand over the *torn notes*, I knew I had to do something. So, I called Kala Bhabhi, this is Seema, my niece, she went in as Sanket's wife to the police station." He pointed and introduced a smiling Seema to Jia.

He continued explaining, "When you and Nandu made a run for it and Tambe chased after you with Gaikwad, Seema quietly pocketed the *torn notes* and brought them to me. I called Ravi at Om Shanti Angadia and asked him to come to Malad with the parcel."

Gaurav then took out one half of the *torn note* from his pocket and handed it over to Ravi and looked at Jia, "Do you have the other half of the '*note*'?"

Jia nodded and retrieved the other half of the torn '*note*' from her purse. She handed it over to Ravi, who placed the two *torn notes* together. They were a perfect match.

"See, everything is in order," Ravi said with a smile.

The group breathed a sigh of relief as they realised that their plan had worked. They had outsmarted Tambe and his constables and were now in possession of the complete $100 *note*.

Meanwhile, at the police station, Tambe was reviewing the footage when he noticed something strange. Seema, the woman who had come into the station crying and claiming to be Sanket's wife, had picked up the *torn notes* and slipped them into her pocket before leaving.

Tambe realised that the *torn notes* were nothing but *tokens* used by the angadias to send and collect valuable parcels containing cash or jewellery. He deduced that the entire charade of Jia and Nandu had been for the *torn note* and that they had been working with the angadias to help them transport valuable items.

While Gaikwad had been fiercely chasing him through the winding lanes of Bhuleshwar, Nandu ran frantically, trying to shake off his pursuer. As he darted through narrow alleys and deftly dodged around the incoming traffic, he became disoriented and lost his sense of direction. He had never been to this part of the city before and had no clue where he was going.

Gaikwad, on the other hand, was intimately familiar with the city's alleys and streets. He was able to anticipate Nandu's movements and stayed one step ahead of him, determined to catch him.

Finally, after what seemed like an interminable chase, Nandu found himself running in circles, completely lost. As he rounded a corner, he was startled to see the police station looming in front of him.

Gaikwad was hot on his heels, and he swiftly overpowered Nandu, handcuffing him. "You're not going anywhere," Gaikwad declared as he led Nandu back to the police station.

As Nandu was brought into the police station, Tambe glared at him and asked, "Did you kill Sanket for the *torn note?*"

A shocked Nandu replied, "*Sahab*, that was a genuine accident. I didn't know anything about the *torn notes* until I overheard Jia and Gaurav talking about it last night."

"Jia, so that's *Sulbhaben's* real name," Tambe asked. "Where were you last night?"

Nandu realised he was cornered. He looked at Tambe and said, "At the garage. I was there with Junaid. I overheard Jia and Gaurav talking later."

Upon hearing Gaurav's name, Tambe looked up and asked, "Gaurav, Shantanu's friend?"

Nandu shook his head. "Never heard of any Shantanu, but Gaurav used to work with Madhav *bhai*."

"Madhav *bhai... Aai chi*," Tambe muttered, slapping his fingers on his forehead. "I should have guessed earlier."

Nandu looked dejected. "I never thought Jia would get involved in something like this."

Tambe glared at him and asked Gaikwad to throw him into the locker. As Gaikwad escorted Nandu out, Tambe suddenly stopped him and asked, "Nandu, you said that Sanket was on the phone when the truck crashed into you, right?"

"Yes," Nandu replied.

Tambe wondered aloud, who might Sanket have been talking to then. He went through Sanket's phone call records and checked the number of the last call. To his surprise, the number belonged to Om Shanti Angadia, a shop that he had heard of before.

Tambe decided to call the number and ask to speak to the proprietor. The operator at Om Shanti Angadia answered the phone.

"Hello, may I speak to the proprietor of the shop?" Tambe asked.

"I'm sorry, Ravi *bhai* is not available at the moment. Can I help you with something else?" The voice at the other end replied.

A frustrated Tambe lost his temper and shouted into the phone, "*Aaye, Malaa Taambae,* Bhuleshwar *Polis Staishan madhil Kaanstaebal Aahe,* I need to speak with Ravi urgently. Do you know when he'll be back?"

"Sir, Ravi *bhai* has gone to his other shop in Malad. I'm not sure when he'll be back," the voice replied politely.

Tambe took out his phone and said, "Give me the phone number and address of the Malad shop."

"I'm sorry, Sir, I can't give you the phone number..." the voice countered cautiously.

Tambe shouted back again, "*hatya adveshana hai,* murder investigation. I need that address now, or I'll come and arrest you on Ravi's behalf and make sure you rot in jail for the rest of your life."

The voice panicked and said, "Okay, fine. 3rd floor, Mehta House, Kanha Mandir Lane, Malad East."

Tambe thanked the operator and hung up the phone, his mind racing with the implications of what he had just learned. He realised that when Jia had managed to escape from the police station – she had likely been in contact with Gaurav and had arranged to meet him at the Malad shop. He was determined to catch them and bring them to justice.

As Nandu and Gaikwad looked on, Tambe rushed into SI Patil's room. A few moments later, both he and SI Patil came out of the room in a hurry. Tambe pointed at Nandu and shouted at Gaikwad and the others, "Throw him into the lockup and follow me."

"Please, Sir, let me come with you," Nandu pleaded with Tambe. "They made a fool of me too, Sir. I can help you by being a witness." Tambe looked at SI Patil for permission, who hesitated for a moment before nodding his head in agreement.

Back at the same time in Malad, Ravi smiled and opened the safe behind him. He took out a small box and handed it to a surprised Gaurav. Jia took the box from Gaurav and opened it. Her face lit up as she saw that it was full of gold biscuits. She smiled gleefully and looked at Ravi and then at Gaurav, who looked at Seema and then at Jia.

"We have to give Seema a 5% commission for the work she did at the police station," Gaurav said sheepishly.

Jia stared at him and then smiled. "For once, I agree with you." Everyone laughed as Jia put the box into her purse.

Gaurav, happy and excited at finally being able to collect the parcel, hugged Ravi and thanked him, while Jia hugged Seema.

Just as they were about to leave the room, there was a knock on the door. Nandu, along with SI Patil, Tambe, and the constables, burst into the room.

"Police! Everyone, run!" Gaurav yelled as he grabbed Jia's hand and started to dash to the back door.

Tambe, his right hand bandaged from his earlier injury, pulled out his gun and aimed it at Gaurav. "Don't move! You're under arrest!" he shouted.

Gaurav and Jia tried to outmanoeuvre Tambe and the constables, dodging nimbly around tables and chairs as they made their way towards the door. Gaurav and Jia were faster and more agile than Tambe, who struggled with the injury on his hand.

As they reached the door, SI Patil took out his gun and fired. The bullet ricocheted off the furniture and struck Gaurav in the shoulder. He stumbled and fell to the ground, yelling in pain.

"Gaurav!" Jia shouted as she stopped abruptly in her tracks.

Tambe and the constables approached Gaurav, ready to apprehend him. But Gaurav, in pain but determined, motioned for Jia to leave. "Go, get out of here!" he yelled.

Jia hesitated for a moment, not wanting to leave Gaurav behind. But she knew that she had to escape if she was going to have any chance of getting help for him. She turned and ran out the door, her heart racing with fear and adrenaline.

Tambe and Nandu both chased after Jia, determined to capture her. They split up, trying to corner her from both ends. Jia was quick on her feet and managed to give Tambe the slip, darting through narrow alleys and dodging around shops. Breathless and exhausted, she collapsed against a wall, trying to catch her breath.

But Nandu was hot on her heels, and he managed to catch up with her. Just as he was about to grab her arm, Jia slipped out of his grasp and ran off again.

She ran as quickly as she could, her feet burning the tar on the road. She could hear his footsteps behind her, growing louder and closer with every passing second.

Just as she thought she couldn't run any further, Jia saw a crowd moving along the road ahead of her. It was a Sikh religious procession, packed with people and music. Jia realised that this was her chance to escape and blend in with the crowd.

She slowed her pace and joined the procession, mingling with the people and trying to avoid detection. Nandu, still following her, tried to push his way through the crowd, but he was slowed down by the press of bodies.

Jia took advantage of the chaos and managed to slip away from Nandu's sight. She ended up sitting in the congregation at the Gurdwara, catching her breath and trying to calm her racing thoughts.

Nandu also followed the procession into the Gurdwara but was unable to locate Jia, eventually he gave up and left the Gurdwara dejectedly. Jia watched him go with a sigh of relief, grateful to have escaped his grasp once again. She knew that she still had a long journey ahead of her and that she had to keep moving to find help for Gaurav and bring him to safety. But for now, at least, she was safe.

Meanwhile, an unconscious and bleeding Gaurav was wheeled into the emergency room of the Cama hospital. The doctors performed emergency surgery and removed the embedded bullet as SI Patil and others waited outside.

Tambe, who had been chasing Jia, finally arrived at the hospital. SI Patil looked at Tambe and motioned for him to follow him out.

"Did you get her?" he asked.

Tambe shook his head and said, "She gave me the slip, but we'll get her. I'm sure she'll call him. They are lovebirds."

SI Patil took a cigarette out of his pocket and said, "You're sure? They're separated and she has what they were looking for. I have a feeling she'll disappear."

Tambe took the lighter out of his pocket and lit up SI Patil's cigarette. "No sir, Nandu was the reason for their separation.

"What about Nandu?" SI Patil asked as he blew out smoke from his lips

"He will also come back. He needs the money as well." Tambe smirked.

Chapter 9

Rendezvous

After narrowly escaping Nandu at the Gurdwara, Jia knew she had to leave Mumbai as soon as possible. She had no destination in mind, but she knew she couldn't stay in the city any longer. She made her way to Mumbai Central railway station and bought a ticket for the next long-distance train heading to Agra, which was leaving in an hour. She hoped that by leaving the city, she could put some distance between herself and Tambe and Nandu, who were both after her.

As she waited for the train to depart, Jia realised she needed to find a way to let Gaurav know what was happening. She knew he was in the hospital and worried he might think she had abandoned him. She considered sending him a message or calling him, but she knew it wasn't safe for her to use the phone. She needed to find a way to communicate with him without alerting Tambe and the others.

She sat on the platform, deep in thought, and then an idea occurred to her. She rummaged through her bag and pulled out a pen and a piece of paper. She scribbled a quick note to Gaurav, explaining where she was going and why. She folded the note and slipped it into an envelope, then wrote Gaurav's name on the front. She looked around, trying to figure out how to get the letter to him.

Just then, she saw an ambulance with "Cama Hospital" written on it. She approached it cautiously. A wheelchair patient was being transferred from the ambulance. As the hospital staff prepared to leave, Jia spotted the same nurse she and Gaurav had met earlier at the hospital whilst they were searching for Sanket.

"Excuse me, ma'am," Jia called out to the nurse as she approached the ambulance. "Could you do me a favour and deliver this letter to a patient in the emergency room at the hospital?"

The nurse hesitated for a moment, looking at the envelope in Jia's outstretched hand. "I'm sorry, but I can't just go around delivering personal letters for people. It's against hospital policy," she said.

Jia's face fell. "Please, it's important. Gaurav, my brother whom you met yesterday, remember, he was injured in the shootout that happened in Malad today morning. The police aren't allowing us to see him. Our mom had a heart scare when she heard about it, and I have to leave to take care of her. I just want to send him a quick note to let him know we're thinking of him."

The nurse softened at the sight of Jia's pleading expression. "Well, I suppose I could make an exception just this once. But you have to promise me you won't ask me to do this again, okay?"

Jia nodded eagerly. "I promise. Thank you so much. And here, please take this as a token of my appreciation," she said, stealthily slipping the nurse some money.

The nurse accepted the envelope and the money with a smile. "I'll make sure to deliver this to Gaurav as soon as I can. Take care now." With that, the nurse turned and headed back into the ambulance.

As Jia watched the ambulance drive away, she hoped her message would reach Gaurav in time. She knew he would be worried about her, and she wanted to let him know she was okay.

Tambe paced the corridor, his mind a whirl of worry for Gaurav's surgery and a fierce determination to catch Jia and bring her to justice. He had a feeling that she would try to leave the city, and he was determined to stop her.

His thoughts were interrupted when he saw a nurse inquiring about Gaurav at the reception desk. His instincts kicked in, and he suspected that the nurse had a message from Jia. He followed her quietly, his heart racing as he tried to stay out of sight so as not to alert her.

The nurse turned and looked around, and Tambe froze, his pulse pounding in his ears. He held his breath, hoping that she wouldn't notice him lurking in the shadows.

Finding nothing amiss, the nurse entered the emergency room. Tambe let out a sigh of relief and crept closer, trying to get a glimpse of what was happening. He saw the nurse approach Gaurav, who was lying in bed, staring blankly at the ceiling. She pretended to check his chart and quickly slipped an envelope into his hand before hurrying out of the room.

Tambe knew he had to act fast. He burst into the room and snatched the letter out of Gaurav's hand, reading its contents with mounting frustration. Jia was planning to take a long-distance train to Agra, and there was no way Tambe could catch her in time. He also knew that Jia had the Angadia's parcel with her, and the only way he could get that was to use Gaurav as leverage.

"What are you doing?" a dejected Gaurav asked, looking up at Tambe

"My job," Tambe replied, "and it looks like she's planning to visit the Taj Mahal in Agra, leaving you behind with us."

Gaurav stared at him blankly. Tambe smiled and then said, "*Mi tula saathi eka deal karnyaacha haka asato*"

What kind of deal?" Gaurav asked sceptically.

"I'll make sure you go free if you help me bring Jia back to the police station," Tambe said, trying to sound as sincere as possible.

"Why should I trust you?" Gaurav asked. "You could just turn me in as soon as we catch her."

Tambe hesitated, knowing that he couldn't reveal the real reason he was making this deal. "Listen, you're a friend of Shantanu's and he asked me to look out for you. I'm doing this because I owe it to him and because I know Nandu is in cahoots with Junaid. I have no sympathy for either of them. Please, Gaurav, I need your help. Together, we can catch Jia and bring her safely back before Nandu and Junaid can do any harm. I'll make sure that both of you become witnesses and walk away free and clear. *Kaya mhanata*? Deal?"

Gaurav hesitated for a moment, then nodded. He knew that he had no choice but to go along with Tambe's plan to rescue Jia. "Okay," he said. "I'll do it. But you have to promise me that you'll let us go."

Tambe nodded. "*Aai shapath*," he said. "Just help me catch her and bring her back safely to the police station."

With the deal struck, Gaurav and Tambe set out to plan their little excursion out of the hospital. They knew that they had to be careful. They couldn't risk alerting constables or SI Patil about their movement, and they had to find a way to catch up with Jia before she left the city.

Gaurav was still recovering from the bullet wound in his shoulder and was in a lot of pain. He leaned heavily on Tambe as they cautiously climbed out of the window, jumped down and made their way through the corridor, trying their best to stay on their feet.

"We have to catch the local," Tambe said, quickly looking around for a taxi to take them to Churchgate. "It's our only chance to catch up with Jia."

Gaurav nodded, gritting his teeth against the pain. He knew that he had to keep moving, no matter how much it hurt.

Tambe hailed a taxi and they rushed down the platform at Churchgate, frantically searching for the local train to Mumbai Central. As they ran, Gaurav's wound started to bleed again, and he felt a wave of dizziness wash over him.

But he fought through it, focusing on the task at hand. He knew that Jia was counting on him, and he couldn't let her down.

Finally, they reached the local train and climbed aboard, taking seats in the back so they could keep an eye on the platform. As the train pulled out of the station, Gaurav leaned back in his seat, trying to catch his breath.

"We have to be ready," Tambe said, eyeing Gaurav with concern. "If the train has already left from Mumbai Central, we will have to catch it at Borivali."

Gaurav nodded, determined to do whatever it took to catch Jia and bring her back safely to the police station. He knew that it wouldn't be easy, but he was ready to do whatever it took to get the job done.

Nandu had kept a watchful eye on the hospital all day. He had seen Tambe and the other constables earnestly maintaining their vigil outside the emergency room. He knew that Jia would contact Gaurav and that she might even show up at the hospital, so he waited.

A few hours later, bored by the endless wait, Nandu went to the tea shop to get a snack. As he ordered, he saw the same nurse who had come out of Gaurav's room walk in with a ward boy. They sat at the table next to him. The nurse looked around and, noticing Nandu staring at them, they got up and changed tables.

Nandu watched the two of them suspiciously as he picked at his Vada pav and tea, trying to overhear their conversation. He quietly took out his phone and switched on the camera, pretending to take a selfie while aiming the camera at them. He was astounded by what he saw: the nurse opened her purse and took out a bundle of notes, which she handed to the ward boy. Nandu strained to hear their conversation and could only make out, "I heard Tambe read the letter... and tore it? Are you sure?"

Nandu's mind processed the information he had heard, and he quickly left his tea and Vada pav unfinished, rushing back to the hospital.

He reached the emergency room only to find that everything was as quiet as before, with the same constables on guard outside the room. Nandu moved cautiously through the corridor towards the room, pacing himself behind a ward boy who was transporting medicine. He quickly crossed the door and went behind the vending machine. He waited, motionless and hidden behind it for a few moments, trying to decide what to do next. As he watched, Gaikwad came out of the room and crossed over to the vending machine. Nandu quickly darted across the door opposite and landed outside near the photocopy shop, just behind the emergency room. Unknowingly, Tambe and Gaurav had just jumped out the window behind him. Nandu continued to watch Gaikwad operate the vending machine and then leave with a bottle of water. He turned to look around and almost screamed when he saw Tambe and Gaurav sneak out of the hospital through the 'C' Gate. He composed himself and ran after them.

As Nandu followed Tambe and Gaurav's trail, his heart pounded out loud. He couldn't shake the feeling that something was off, and he was determined to find out what was going on. He had thought Tambe was an upright constable, but now he wasn't so sure. He watched as both men got into a taxi for Churchgate.

He couldn't understand why Tambe would be on a local train with an injured Gaurav when he could have directly taken the taxi to wherever they were going. He couldn't shake the feeling that Jia was at the centre of it all.

At Churchgate, as Tambe and Gaurav boarded the train, Nandu climbed into the adjoining coach, his pulse pounding in his ears. As the train began to move, Nandu's thoughts were interrupted by a hand on his shoulder. He turned to see Junaid and his boys; their faces grim.

Junaid motioned for him to sit down on the empty seats. He told his boys to keep an eye out for Tambe and Gaurav, "Let me know when they're ready to get off," and then sat down next to Nandu.

"Nandu," Junaid said, his voice laced with anger. "We have a problem. You and Jia already owed us a lot of money, and yesterday night the loan amount went up, we want all of it back."

Nandu's heart sank with fear. He had hoped he could escape Junaid and his gang, but it seemed that he was doomed to be stuck with them forever.

"I don't have any money, Junaid *bhai*, I gave you whatever I had yesterday night itself," Nandu said, trying to plead his case. "I've just managed to escape from Tambe, and I almost died in the shootout at your place."

Junaid snorted. "Tambe, huh? We've been keeping an eye on all of you. What is Tambe doing with Gaurav on a local train, with you following them? Do you think we are all idiots? Something's up, and we want you to find out what it is. Find out where Jia is, and bring us the money she owes us."

Nandu hesitated, knowing he was in a tough position. If he didn't do as Junaid asked, he would be dead. He knew he had no choice. He nodded; his heart filled with fear. "Okay, Junaid *bhai*. I'll do it. But you have to promise me that you'll let me go once I bring you the money."

Junaid grinned, his teeth glinting in the dim light of the train. "Sure, just return us the money you and Jia owe, and you'll be free to go."

As the train slowed down, one of Junaid's boys interrupted their conversation, "They're getting ready to get off. Mumbai Central."

Junaid got up and patted Nandu on his back. "Go get the money, and don't forget we're watching you."

With a heavy heart, Nandu got off the train and followed Tambe and Gaurav, determined to find Jia and bring her back to Junaid and his boys. He had no other choice. It was either that or face the dire consequences that Junaid had threatened him with.

As he walked away, Nandu could feel Junaid's eyes on him, watching his every move. The fear was palpable, and he knew that he had to be careful if he wanted to make it out of the situation alive.

Chapter 10

The Train

As Jia sat in the second-class AC coach of the train to Agra, she couldn't shake the feeling that something was amiss. She had hoped against hope that Gaurav would make it to the train in time, but as the minutes ticked by, she knew it was expecting too much.

Just then, a man sat down next to her. Jia looked at him warily, her hand instinctively going to the box of gold hidden in her bag.

"Don't be afraid," the man said, noticing her nervousness. "I'm here to help you."

Jia relaxed slightly, but she remained wary. "Who are you?" she asked.

"My name is Hari. Ravi *bhai* sent me," the man replied. "I'm a friend of Gaurav's. He asked me to help you get out of the city."

Jia's eyes widened in surprise. "Gaurav asked you to help me?"

Hari nodded. "He knew you were in danger and wanted to make sure you were safe. He gave me this to give to you," he said, pulling out a $100 '*note*'. He tore it into half and handed one half to Jia along with an envelope.

She hesitated for a moment before reaching into her bag and taking out the box of gold. She handed it to Hari, who nodded in satisfaction.

"Thank you," she said, her voice choked with emotion.

"Thank Ravi *bhai*," Hari said, smiling. "I'm just glad we could help. Now, you need to get off this train and find another one. Go someplace peaceful and wait. It will calm you down. I have a feeling that Tambe and Nandu won't give up easily."

As Hari left the coach, Jia opened her purse and retrieved half of the original $100 '*note*' which they had exchanged with Sanket's parcel. She stuck the new half to it and put it back in her purse.

The train's horn blared, signalling that it was about to depart. Jia looked out the window, hoping for a last glimpse of Gaurav. But as the train began to move, she knew he wasn't coming.

With a heavy heart, Jia made her way to the door of the coach. As she stepped onto the platform, Hari's words rang in her head: "Go someplace peaceful and wait. It will calm you down."

She gasped and looked around, then turned and climbed up the stairs, crossing the bridge to the other platform. There, she saw what Hari had meant and knew that was where she had to go. The train to Amritsar was ready to depart.

Unknowingly to her, Tambe and Gaurav had boarded the train to Agra, while Nandu had followed them. But Jia had managed to outsmart them all and get onto the train to Amritsar without them realising it.

As the train pulled away from the station, Jia leaned back against the seat and closed her eyes, feeling exhausted from the events of the past few days. However, as the miles ticked by, she couldn't shake the feeling that she was being followed. She knew she was being paranoid, but she couldn't help looking over her shoulder every few minutes, expecting to see Tambe or Nandu standing there.

As the sun began to set, Jia started to doze off. She was awoken by the sound of someone sitting down next to her and opened her eyes to see Gaurav there, looking relieved.

"Gaurav!" she exclaimed, surprised and happy to see him. She threw her arms around him and hugged him tightly. "I can't believe you're here! I was so worried about you – thank God you're safe."

"Tambe sent me to bring you back," he replied, hugging her back. "He made a deal with me. If I helped him catch you, he would let me go."

Jia's heart sank. She had hoped that Gaurav would be on her side, but it seemed that he had chosen Tambe over her.

"I'm sorry, Jia," Gaurav said, seeing the look of disappointment on her face. "I had to see the expression on your face. But I promise you, I'll do everything I can to help us escape. You have no idea what all I had to do to get rid of Tambe – he is safely on his way to Agra now."

Jia laughed and kissed him on the cheek. "You always know how to make me laugh," she said. "I'm just glad you're here with me now."

"Where's the box?" Gaurav asked, his voice laced with concern.

Jia's face went sombre, and Gaurav knew something was wrong. "When I was running from the police, I dropped it," she admitted.

Gaurav looked around the coach, aghast. "What are we going to do now?" he asked, his panic rising.

But Jia just laughed and patted his shoulder. "Got you, didn't I? I said I'd get you. Don't worry, it's safe. We just have to give them this *'note'*." She took the $100 bill out of her purse and showed him.

Gaurav laughed too, relieved that the situation wasn't as dire as he had thought. "So, Ravi managed to send someone to you," he said, still shaking his head as Jia put the $100 bill back in her purse. She put an arm around Gaurav and hugged him hard.

Together, they hatched a plan to stay safe from Tambe and Nandu and start a new life. They knew it wasn't the ideal situation they were in, but with each other's help, they were determined to make it work, no matter what obstacles lay ahead.

www.ingramcontent.com/pod-product-compliance
Lightning Source LLC
La Vergne TN
LVHW091101150826
845673LV00002B/668